PRAISE

"With a quai... Penny's Thre... Kerry Greenwood... Jacqueline Winspear's Maisie Dobbs, this mystery series has it all!" —Murder by the Book, Texas

"Highly entertaining... fans and newcomers alike will find lots to love." —*Publishers Weekly*, Starred Review

"Well plotted and laced with dry wit, Lane's adventures are entirely satisfying summer reading." —Shelf Awareness

"There are days when nothing suits a reader like a good old-fashioned classic cozy with a puzzle plot, a country setting and some nice slight characters. When that urge strikes, Iona Whishaw's delightful BC series featuring Lane Winslow and, now, husband, Inspector Darling of the King's Cove constabulary, are just the ticket." —*Globe and Mail*

"The setting is fresh and the cast endearing." —CrimeReads

"Brave, bold and brilliant, Lane Winslow is a force to be reckoned with." —*Toronto Star*

"As always, Whishaw's characters are the heart of the whodunit—we adored spending time with Lane and her entourage, from the wisecracking Inspector Darling to his quirky but highly skilled crew of constables." —Apple Books

"It's the perfect series for fans of Miss Fisher and Maisie Dobbs." —*Zoomer* magazine

PRAISE FOR THE LANE WINSLOW MYSTERIES

"Very charming and delightful. If you like Louise Penny's novels, this is right up your street." —CBC Ontario Morning

"Think a young Katharine Hepburn—beautiful, smart and beyond capable. Winslow is an example of the kind of woman who emerged after the war, a confident female who had worked in factories building tanks and guns, a woman who hadn't yet been suffocated by the 1950s perfect housewife ideal." —*Vancouver Sun*

"I absolutely love the modern sensibility of these novels, of their feminism, sense of justice, their anti-racism, their progressiveness, which somehow never seems out of place in a tiny BC hamlet in 1948." —Kerry Clare, author of *Waiting for a Star to Fall* and editor of 49th Shelf

"Iona Whishaw's writing is worthy of taking its place alongside the works of Agatha Christie and Dorothy L Sayers... deftly crafted and briskly paced." —Fiona Valpy, author of *The Dressmaker's Gift*

"What a delight!... crafted with such charming finesse that readers will fall in love as I did." —Genevieve Graham, #1 *USA Today* bestselling author of *Bluebird*

"An engaging, superbly crafted page turner of a mystery." —Alan Hlad, international and *USA Today* bestselling author of *The Long Flight Home*

"Stellar..." —Eliza Knight, *USA Today* bestselling author of *Starring Adele Astaire*

A SEASON FOR SPIES

THE LANE WINSLOW MYSTERY SERIES

A Season For Spies

A Killer in King's Cove
Death in a Darkening Mist
An Old, Cold Grave
It Begins in Betrayal
A Sorrowful Sanctuary
A Deceptive Devotion
A Match Made for Murder
A Lethal Lesson
Framed in Fire
To Track a Traitor
Lightning Strikes the Silence
The Cost of a Hostage

IONA WHISHAW

A SEASON FOR SPIES

A LANE WINSLOW PREQUEL

TOUCHWOOD

Copyright © 2025 by Iona Whishaw

All rights reserved. No part of this publication may be reproduced, stored in a retrieval system, or transmitted in any form or by any means—electronic, mechanical, audio recording, or otherwise, including those for text and data mining, AI training, and similar technologies—without the written permission of the publisher or a photocopying licence from Access Copyright. Permissions and licensing contribute to a secure and vibrant book industry by helping to support writers and publishers through the purchase of authorized editions and excerpts. To obtain an official licence, please visit accesscopyright.ca.

For more information, contact the publisher at:

TouchWood Editions
touchwoodeditions.com

This book is a work of fiction. Names, characters, places, and incidents are either products of the author's imagination or are used fictitiously. Any resemblance to actual events or locales or persons, living or dead, is entirely coincidental.

Edited by Claire Philipson
Cover illustration by Margaret Hanson

CATALOGUING DATA AVAILABLE FROM LIBRARY AND ARCHIVES CANADA
ISBN 9781771514910 (Indigo exclusive softcover)
ISBN 9781771514828 (softcover)
ISBN 9781771514835 (electronic)
ISBN 9781771514842 (audiobook)

TouchWood Editions acknowledges that the land on which we live and work is within the traditional territories of the Lkwungen (Esquimalt and Songhees), Malahat, Pacheedaht, Scia'new, T'Sou-ke, and W̱SÁNEĆ (Pauquachin, Tsartlip, Tsawout, and Tseycum) peoples.

We acknowledge the financial support of the Government of Canada through the Canada Book Fund and the Canada Council for the Arts, and of the Province of British Columbia through the British Columbia Arts Council and the Book Publishing Tax Credit.

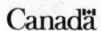

This book was produced using FSC®-certified, acid-free papers, processed chlorine free, and printed with soya-based inks.

PRINTED IN CANADA

29 28 27 26 25   1 2 3 4 5

To all the women in intelligence in the Second World War,
who risked everything to prove they belong.

PROLOGUE

SHE WATCHED, HER LIPS CLAMPED in frustration, as the Jeep crawled with agonizing slowness up the road. It would be dark soon, and the temperature had dropped, freezing the slush on the road and delivering more snow—this time icy needles that cut into the exposed parts of her face. The road climbed past the wood toward where she was standing now on the top of the hill. Her hours of waiting had finally paid off. She could see them now. This was what she'd been waiting for.

She pulled the log down the short hill from the edge of the wood, her hands almost frozen, whispering a thanks to the woodcutter who'd left it behind, and pushed and pulled until it lay across the narrow road. She wouldn't even have to hide it under the snow. It would stop the Jeep, and someone would have to get out and move it. That was all the time she'd need. Breathing hard from the effort of manoeuvring the log into place, she crouched low behind a hump of snow and waited, her Beretta at the ready. She shivered, angry. He'd bungled it and got himself captured, jeopardizing their mission. No matter. She would free him, and they would get the traitor. She nodded several times, feeling a heady sense of triumph. They would get him.

CHAPTER ONE

December 20, 1940

"THIS IS ABYSMAL," LANE WINSLOW said, shuddering and picking her way over debris along the Strand this icy morning. A building in ruins across the road was still smoking, and a mother with a small girl was disconsolately picking through the rubble. The morning was damp and grey, and the acrid smell of bomb sites was becoming all too familiar. "Shouldn't that little girl have been sent to the country with the other children?" Lane shivered. "It's diabolical that they bomb every bloody night. You can't even get your feet under you."

Lane and her fellow translator and flatmate, Irene, were in search of a cup of tea and something for breakfast before they had to be at headquarters in two hours for a briefing. The weather was disheartening, the worst in recent years. The rain had stopped, but the temperature was bitingly cold. Their usual teashop along the Strand was full to bursting, so they were looking for a quieter place away from the river up along Carey Street. There was a heightened mood on the streets, Lane thought. Was it because the cold reminded people that Christmas was coming, and they were desperately hanging on to anything they could feel good about?

"I am tired of having to be plucky, I must say, and I haven't even had a bomb drop on me. It's the constant strain of worrying, I think," Irene said. "I'm gasping for a cuppa. Look, how about here?"

The little café was more than half full, and the warm fug of damp wool and smoke clung in the air, but there was a tiny table at the back, and they collapsed gratefully into the chairs. Almost everyone was in uniform, except for a couple of older women who perched on either side of a corner table looking like two piles of wool coats. A harried woman with a tray in her hand signalled that she'd be right over.

"Why are there so many people in every place?" Lane wondered, shrugging off her own damp coat. "I thought it might be some sort of desperate bid for Christmas spirit, but now I'm wondering if everyone senses that with petrol and sugar rationed everything else can't be far behind, so they're all frantically grabbing the last decent bun."

"Well, if there's to be a last decent bun, it's mine, along with a fried egg," Irene declared, taking off her gloves and rubbing her hands together. People were talking and even laughing, giving the place the cheer that comes with getting out of the cold and having a hot mug of tea between one's hands. "Think of all the toffs over at the Ritz. I bet they aren't enjoying their tea as much as these people are. There's nothing like a cup of tea and a breakfast that you've really earned!" Irene was showing signs of good spirits. She'd been away from the flat again last night. Another new beau? Lane wondered.

Lane smiled. I suppose we have earned our tea, she thought, bent for long hours over communications that needed translating and sorting. Rushing down to huddle in the basement when the sirens went. Everyone in the city had earned a good breakfast, she thought, under those criteria.

"What'll it be, ladies?" The woman with the tray had sidled her considerable figure through the crowded tables and was now beside them.

"A large pot of tea, any kind of buns you have, and can we have fried eggs?" Lane asked.

"You can have a fried egg apiece," the woman said. "They aren't rationed yet, but they're harder to get."

"Splendid!" said Irene. "And no root vegetables of any kind!"

"Oh, I know," the woman said. "We'll all be sitting in the Underground eating raw turnips if Herr Hitler keeps this up! I can do you a little sugar and some milk for your tea, though."

"See, everyone is being plucky. It's our national duty. We can't let the side down," Lane said, when the woman had left. "Though I think I draw the line at rushing up to the roof to watch the bombing. Katie did that the other night and said it was thrilling."

"I don't know. It would make a change from cowering underground. What do you think Barking is going to tell us?" Irene asked, referring to their commanding officer, Barkley.

"It won't be 'run along and get your hair done and buy a new frock,' that's for sure," Lane answered.

"Is that what you'd secretly like to be doing? I'd like to

go into a fabulous restaurant and have an enormous meal, with plenty of gravy, without the windows blowing out and having to duck under the table," Irene said dreamily.

Lane smiled. "I thought you didn't like toffs? Getting my hair done and a new frock would be rather nice, now I think of it. And the meal, of course, too. I never used to think about that sort of thing much. I was much too busy studying. Now I crave frivolity."

Irene shook her head. "I mean, I ask you . . . did you see that quiz in the Kensington paper today? 'What are the two most important root vegetables?' A less frivolous thing would be difficult to imagine. Newspaper quizzes are supposed to be fun!"

Lane sighed. "I suppose with people losing their houses and all those people dying every night, it's good to have root vegetables to distract one. What are they, anyway?"

"I don't know. Potatoes and beetroot? Carrots and turnips?"

"You didn't turn the page to find out?" Lane asked.

"I think it's carrots. Good for night vision. Good for looking at documents in bad lighting."

Lane shook her head. Irene didn't always remember not to talk about their work. And she smoked. She pulled out her little brass cigarette case now and offered it to Lane, who declined.

"You should take it up," Irene said, striking a match. "It's the only thing in this awful weather."

The pot of tea arrived, and the two young women fell on it gratefully. It was even decently strong. Lane watched pretty blond Irene with her cigarette in one hand and her cup in the other and wondered about her own life. At first the service had seemed a bit like school—everyone there for the same purpose—and she imagined that she would develop new friendships, but in fact they all knew very little about each other. Nevertheless, they could get close, because they were in a rarified atmosphere where no one else knew what they were doing. It made for camaraderie, but it could be hazardous. She'd learned this to her cost when she'd met Danielle, a girl her age whom she had rather liked because she read and had something to say. Within two months of Lane meeting her, she'd died when her rooming house was bombed. It was a continuous source of sadness for Lane. She wondered about Danielle's people, and how much they must miss her. She truly feared what her own death might mean to her grandparents, who had doted on both her and her sister all their lives. Well, it was war. One had to pull oneself together. Those same grandparents had taught her that, and taught her well. She sighed and looked at Irene across from her, slurping tea.

She was pretty sure Irene didn't read many books, but she always had something to say based on the women's magazines. She'd come, Lane was sure, from quite a working-class background, but she'd lived in Germany with an aunt after her parents had died, and she read and spoke German well.

"You know that Iris? She's carrying on with a married man!" Irene said suddenly, leaning forward.

Lane sighed. Irene and her gossip. She was incorrigible. "How could you know that?" she asked. "There is no indication of that at all at work."

Irene tapped the side of her nose. "I keep my eye peeled," she said with a wink. "My fella is off away," she added with a sigh. "Africa, I think. He doesn't tell me because he doesn't like to worry me, but of course, we know, don't we? We read things every day about what's going on out there. I can't think how worried he'd be if he knew I knew! What about yours?"

Lane had a fella, of sorts, but she was not allowed to talk about Angus. And she hadn't seen him since early November. She suspected he knew what she did. She sighed at how often she longed to see him. He was something quite high up, she was sure, though he never said. No one ever said anything, she thought, except maybe Irene. "I don't actually have anyone," she said. But she looked at Irene. If she had a fella in Africa, where was she going on the nights she was away?

Irene waved a disbelieving hand. "A pretty girl like you? I don't believe it! They must be queuing up!" She stubbed out her cigarette as their breakfast appeared. "Oh, God, look at this! It's heavenly!"

Lane nodded. It was heavenly indeed. And she was spared having to talk any more about men. She doubted anyone was queuing up for her. She hadn't the capacity for the kind of cheeriness that made Irene fun to be around. She never, she thought, ended any sentences with exclamation marks, and Irene seemed incapable of ending one any other way. Irene, she decided, was quite capable of not letting any grass grow under her feet, beau-wise!

"Do you think they'll let us go home for Christmas?"

"No, I don't," Lane said truthfully. She'd love to go

to her grandparents. She missed them and worried about them. This cold winter had brought heavy snow all over the north, which had brought nearly everything to a standstill, and though her grandmother, another plucky customer, wrote cheery letters about how lovely it was, the border country was well and truly in a deep freeze.

"No, you're right," Irene said with disappointment.

Fuller and a bit happier, the two women left the café and made their way to headquarters. Though the sun had put in an anemic appearance, the temperature had dropped. The shops they passed were contributing what they could to the season. Old posters of Father Christmas from before the war had been dusted off and put in windows, along with a few ornaments and pictures of impossible Christmas dinners served up under fairy-lit trees.

"Look," Lane said, pointing to a sign in the window of a small post office. "They want us to post cards by the twentieth. That's today. I've posted a sum total of two, and they were very sad specimens. My grandparents no doubt have theirs on the mantel in Scotland in pride of place. I doubt my sister's card made it safely to South Africa, though I posted it a month ago."

"I didn't know your grandparents were Scottish, or that you had a sister in Africa," Irene said.

"They're not really Scottish. But they've retired to a nice quiet corner of Scotland. It's so out of the way that aside from the rationing, I doubt this war will ever find them there. They used to live on the continent. As for my sister, my father let her travel to South Africa with a school friend to wait out the war."

"I only have a great-aunt still alive in Ealing," Irene sighed. "She has a good neighbour, so I suppose she won't be completely alone at Christmas. And damn! I've not sent a card. Wait here while I run in and see if they have any, then I can get it out in time. I'd hate to be the reason she has a miserable Christmas!"

"You know, Christmas has a way of being magical no matter the circumstances," Lane said, surprising herself with her own bit of frivolity, albeit sombre. She watched from the pavement as Irene ran into the post office, and then, smiling, stepped aside to let someone through. Then Lane frowned. Hadn't Irene told her before it was an uncle in Ealing? She shook her head. Was half of what Irene said even true?

CHAPTER TWO

"**LIKE THE OLD BIDDIES LIKE** to say, 'There's a war on,' so sorry, no leave. Run along and enjoy what you can till you're wanted. Sorry. No Father Christmas this year," Barkley concluded, looking like he was pleased no one would be getting a Christmas.

Lane looked at Irene and rolled her eyes. They'd been sitting in the back row, Lane on principle—she hated to sit in the front row of anything. There was the sound of chairs being pushed about as the small group of fifteen got up and prepared to leave. Conversation was quietly disconsolate. Lane wanted to go, but Irene took that moment to lean forward and flirt with the man in front of her, blocking the way. Lane stood, waiting, trying not to appear rudely impatient, though she felt both rude and impatient. Finally, Irene got up and started for the door. They'd agreed to go shopping for what gifts they might be able to find in the shops, no matter what they heard at this briefing. This little pleasure seemed more imperative than ever now, but as it turned out, it was another thing that was not to be.

"Not you, Winslow." The CO's voice cut through the chatter and brought her up short. Most of the people were out of the room, but those few who were left looked at each other with their eyebrows raised. Winslow appeared to be in trouble. Irene shrugged, waggled her fingers at Lane, saying, "See you when I see you," and disappeared with the rest. Lane watched her go.

Irene was always disappearing, even overnight. Lane appreciated having the little flat to herself, but did wonder at Irene's endless string of boyfriends, "fella" in Africa notwithstanding.

No one wanted to be caught in whatever riptide Lane was in, and she soon found herself alone with the co.

"Sir?"

"Sit down, Winslow." He pointed at the chair directly opposite his desk in the front row. Lane sat, her hands in her lap, her mind running over what might be amiss. She could come up with no real transgression on her part, but her heart was racing, nonetheless. The oh, so aptly named Barkley wasn't one of those avuncular cos dressed in tweeds, who sat back smoking a pipe with nice-smelling tobacco, being comforting and supportive. He had a disagreeable pencil moustache and smoked some horrible brand of gaspers, and he actually barked.

"I can't believe what I'm about to say to you, Winslow. In fact, you're the last person I'd be speaking to if I had any other option."

Encouraging start, Lane thought. "Sir?"

He stood at his desk with his hands behind his back. "You have people in Scotland, don't you?"

"Sir, yes. My grandparents. They've only been there since May. Broughton."

"Good. I want you to go spend Christmas with them."

"Sir?" Now she was completely baffled. She thought she'd blotted her copybook, or at best would be getting some ghastly new assignment. But this? No one else was getting to visit family at Christmas. She couldn't imagine the resentment it would cause.

"That will be agreeable, won't it? Have you been to their cottage?"

So, he knew they lived in a cottage. If she ever did get into any trouble there'd be no hiding! "Yes, sir. Once, to help settle them in."

"Splendid. You got leave for that, I recall." He turned to the wall where a series of maps sat in a stacked holder and looked at the corner of each one. Finding what he wanted, he pulled down a map of Scotland.

Lane's heart sank. She had a feeling this wasn't going to be a nice little Christmas visit to her grandparents after all. He'd taken up his pointer and was pointing at the southeast coast of Scotland, and then, as if he'd changed his mind, he put down his pointer and turned back to her, sitting down in his chair behind the desk.

"Make sure the damn door is closed," he said, opening his cigarette case.

She could see that it was, but she obligingly got up and pulled at the doorknob to confirm. Then she heard a noise. It seemed to come from just outside the door. She opened the door a crack and heard someone moving rapidly down the hall, but when she looked, she could see no one. She shook her head and closed the door again. No doubt one of her nosy workmates wanting to hear just how much trouble she might be in.

"What is it?"

"I thought I heard someone outside, but they're gone."

"I suppose you're as jumpy as all the rest of the girls."

"No, sir, I don't think any of us is very jumpy. You wanted the door closed and I thought that meant you didn't want to be overheard."

He made an indeterminate noise and held out his cigarette case in a half-hearted manner, and when she shook her head, slipped it back in his pocket and lit his cigarette. "Good. Sit down." He waited until she had, and then leaned over toward her, blowing smoke out of the side of his mouth. "I'm going to be frank with you. I'm not sure if what I'm about to tell you is a good idea. If it had been left to me, it would never have been considered." He cleared his throat and heaved a great sigh. "We've got a little job away from your usual desk. A sort of courier job, really. We need to keep it very low-key, and sending a woman would arouse less suspicion."

Lane frowned. Courier? That's what her father called himself, though everyone knew he was a full-blown spy. She wondered if whoever had suggested her knew about her father. If they thought she'd learned anything from him, they were to be sadly mistaken!

"Sir?"

"We just want you to pick someone up. This mission will be need to know only, do you understand?"

"Mission, sir?" This sounded well beyond anything she ever imagined doing.

"Perhaps I shouldn't have said 'mission.' No need to

make heavy weather of it. It's a simple task, really. I want you to meet someone off the east coast of Scotland and take him home to a nice Christmas with your grandparents. Nothing easier."

"Sir?" He was overselling the simplicity of it, she was sure.

"I do wish you'd stop saying 'sir' in that inane way." He sighed again as if he was overcoming an almost overwhelming reluctance to assign her to anything, let alone this job. He leaned over and opened the bottom drawer of the oak desk. "You'll need this." He pulled up a Webley revolver with a silencer and plunked it on the desk. He followed it with a notebook. "Sign for it here. And try not to lose it," he added with exaggerated weariness.

Lane almost recoiled. A revolver? "Why, sir? If I'm just meeting someone?"

"Because, Winslow, there might be a cock-up, we might have got bad information, he might not be who he says he is, he might have been rumbled, there might be a secret cell here that's keeping an eye on things. Because I'm having to send a twenty-year-old girl instead of someone . . . well, experienced, and male. Any number of things. You just have to avoid shooting the target. Or anyone, if you can help it. This whole thing has to be done very much on the q.t."

She imagined turning up at her grandparents' cottage armed to the teeth, or being obliged to actually shoot someone. She sighed, trying to understand the true scope of what he was asking her. She signed next to the date and sat back. "When is the rendezvous, sir, and where?"

He nodded, relieved that she wasn't going to throw up any more objections. "That's more like it." He turned and pointed at the map. "The 'where' is here." He jabbed at the east coast again with his pointer along the borders. "Just south of a fishing village called Eyemouth. A tiny hamlet . . . not even that . . . a couple of cottages . . . called Armuth. Just south, here, there are a number of rocky coves. Twenty-four December, 0100. The Germans are usually pretty accurate."

"Germans, sir? Is the man German?" Lane asked, surprised. Well, of course German. Why else all the secrecy?

He ignored her. "I have an ordnance map of the area." Another drawer, and a folded map appeared. He spread it out on the desk. He'd left his gasper in the ashtray, creating a stream of smoke. "You see here? X marks the spot."

She had got up and was leaning over the desk, and a momentary smile at the old pirate expression crossed her lips. X did indeed mark the spot. A small red X indicated one of a number of coves just south of the hamlet. She scanned the approach. Nothing in the way of a road, certainly, or even a walking path.

"You'll take the local bus and then walk in. The weather has thrown a bit of a spanner into the works. The whole north has shut down because of the sudden heavy snow. If traffic is still closed down when you get there, you'll have to improvise. We have snowshoes for you, just in case. You're a visitor going on a ramble. Your cover, should you be asked where you're going, is that you are going to your grandparents' for Christmas, but meeting a cousin for a Scottish Borders walk first. You've heard the coast is beautiful. You have leave from your job as a secretary for a small firm, say, accountancy. When you've collected the man, he is your fiancé."

She nodded. Her cover of being on a walking holiday in that sort of weather seemed ridiculous. "Snowshoes, sir?"

Barkley stood up and opened a cupboard, pulling out a small well-travelled suitcase, if the stickers were to be believed. He plunked it on the desk, snapped open the clasps, and turned it for Lane to see the contents. Sitting in the bottom of the suitcase was a pair of stubby snowshoes, roughly eighteen inches long and half that wide. "Nifty, eh? You like winter sports."

How had he known that? "As it happens, I do. These look Norwegian."

"Aren't you clever. Yank, if you can believe it. This will be your little valise. We've added a particularly cunning little high-powered torch, here." He pulled out a sleek black torch that was small enough to slide into her pocket. "An Ever Ready Bullseye. I've seen from your dossier you know Morse code. You may need it. You will, of course, keep it and the Webley hidden and handy in that leather bag of yours."

Morse code? She hoped she remembered it as well as he thought. "Does he speak English, my fiancé?"

"Some. Speaks Polish and German. You speak German. That's the point of sending you on this job. The only point, frankly." Lane thought the last remark entirely unnecessary and was beginning to rebel under his palpable doubt.

"He's Polish? I should think it would raise suspicion if we were wandering around the countryside speaking German."

"Yes, so don't. You'll have to think of something."

"I should let my grandparents know. They are on

the telephone."

"No telephone. You'll send a wire. 'Marc and I will see you at Christmas.'"

Whatever would they make of that? Lane wondered. "How is he getting here, sir?"

"Submarine will drop him in a dinghy out at sea. Usually, their subs are far up on the northern coast, but I suspect the whole coast is littered with Germans and Poles and even Norwegians who've been spying for the enemy and fetching up here mostly by parachute, but by sea as well. They may signal to make sure their man landed. Be ready to respond. Normally, the people they send over are completely inept, and we pick them up immediately. What we don't know is how many have succeeded. This one is ours, and most importantly, he has the names of every German agent in the country. And I don't want him lost, do you understand?" He glared fiercely at her, as if she was bound to botch the whole thing. "Now listen. You're to talk to no one or do anything to raise suspicion. Do not let anyone see your revolver or your maps. Do you understand? For all intents and purposes, you are a little secretary going for a short winter holiday and combining it with Christmas at your grandparents'."

Lane sat silently for a few moments. She understood perfectly. This was, for all intents and purposes, a spy mission. She wasn't doing the spying, of course, God forbid, but there was plenty of cloak and dagger. Well, she'd seen her father pretend for years to be nothing but a businessman. She'd had modelling for the role. But it was mad! Who on earth had instructed Barkley to pull a translator off the job to do this?

Barkley had taken up his cigarette and was blowing smoke out of nose and mouth. Finally, she realized what was troubling her. "What if the other side knows he's working for us and sends someone of their own to collect him? Or they arrest him before he's even left?"

"That's not an entirely ridiculous question. And the answer is, we're pretty certain. He's been feeding us information for several months and we've been able to hoover up every known sympathizer in the area, so we don't expect there'll be a reception committee. As to the Germans who come over trying to pretend they're English, they give themselves away immediately, so they don't survive on the loose for more than a day. Trust me, there will be no one there to pick him up but you. It's critical you get him first and not some zealous farmer who thinks he snagged a Nazi. He's called Marc Nowak, and he's a double X. I can't say more than that, and I can't explain what that is." But she knew. Double X referred to the people who did counter espionage. "If he's arrested before he even boards the sub, well, then he won't be there. Nothing we can do about that."

"Why does he have to come here? Can he not stay on wherever he is, doing whatever he does?"

He stubbed out his gasper. "It's got too hot. We want him back here and we'll have him drop out of sight and reassign him. Your password is 'I think I've hurt my bloody ankle.' His is 'Let me have a look.'"

"He speaks enough English for that."

"For God's sake, Winslow! Go get ready. Good practical clothes, trousers if you have them, small leather shoulder bag. That one you have is good. Train to Edinburgh first thing in the morning, overnight in Edinburgh, bus east to the coast, overnight in Eyemouth, walk the last couple of miles to Armuth on the night of the twenty-third, pickup at 0100. If the conditions prohibit this, then I'm afraid you'll have to extemporize. Your best first stop is the White Hart just outside Edinburgh on the road to the coast. Check in there. You've got tomorrow to get to Edinburgh, and the next two days only to get in position if the roads are impassable or there is some other contingency."

What contingencies was he imagining? Lane thought nervously. "What do I do when I've got him to the cottage? How will I get him to the cottage?"

"He's been provided with an RAF uniform. We'll have to hope it's not the usual incompetent German effort, and that this one passes muster. Most of the other spies we've picked up were spotted instantly because of their badly copied uniforms. If anyone asks, he's got shellshock, and let's say he can't speak. You're taking him home. Go on regular transport if you can. There's a bus once a day from Eyemouth back west to Broughton. Failing that because of the roads, back to Edinburgh, then bus to Broughton."

"And when I have him at the cottage?"

"Bring him back here on Christmas night, Boxing Day at the latest. I should have thought that would be obvious to the meanest intelligence." The CO had become impatient.

"Yes, sir." Lane got up, saluted, and started toward the door.

"Don't forget those," he said, nodding his head in the direction of the revolver and the suitcase, as if they were explosives he didn't want to touch.

She turned back, picked up the revolver, and slid it into her leather bag, along with the torch. He opened the bottom drawer again, took out a small box of ammunition, and pushed it across to her. "You might need this as well. And Winslow, try to get this man back in one piece."

Not even a good luck! She hoped it wasn't an indication of how hopeless he thought the expedition was.

Barkley sat for long moments after Lane had left, then sighed and shook his head. She was clever, no doubt, but she was a woman, and women had no place in the intelligence business, especially one as young as that. He'd been arguing against it since the idea first came up. Well, his was not to reason why. Some blighter higher up had reason to think she was the one for the job. On their head be it.

CHAPTER THREE

LANE STOOD ON THE STREET, her ears still ringing, her heart pounding. What on earth possessed them to enlist her for this? Her face was icy from the shock of the frigid air. Blimey, it was cold! She'd have to hurry home to pack. She crossed her fingers that they wouldn't have to go into an air raid shelter in the middle of the night. Scotland, to pick up a spy! The whole thing felt quite unreal. She started homeward, but then thought, if she was going to see her grandparents, she ought to get a couple of little presents. If she had presents with her, that would certainly create some verisimilitude about what she was up to. Provide a cover. She tried to imagine who on earth would challenge her, demand to know where she was going and what she was doing. She almost laughed out loud at the ridiculous notion of needing a cover.

She still had plenty of day left. It would cheer her up to shop and help her put the world to rights after her shock. She hadn't expected to see them at all this Christmas, so she'd go all out.

She looked at the suitcase and muttered a silent curse. She couldn't go around town with a gun and suitcase.

She would have to go back and leave them at the flat. Consequently, she turned toward Theobalds Road, where she and Irene shared a bedsit.

The place was empty. She pushed the suitcase under her bed and looked around for a place to put the revolver. She trusted Irene, but didn't want to leave the gun anywhere that Irene might find it and ask questions. In the end, she decided to push it under her mattress, along with the box of ammunition, and at the last minute, the map. Feeling a sense of unease about the whole thing, she went back into the street to consider her Christmas shopping trip, an activity that felt completely specious, considering what she was about to do.

She would have liked to go to Selfridges, but it had been badly damaged by the horrendous blitz bombing in September. Most of the windows were bricked up and the few displays were war themed. Selfridges, John Lewis, all the department stores along Oxford Street had been bombed. Of course, the intrepid staff had been back on the job within days, cleaning up, keeping what sections of the stores open that they could. She was most sad about the rooftop at Selfridges. She had been taken there once by Angus and it had been gaspingly lovely. Heady drinks, delicious food, majestic views of London, a garden oasis. She shook her head. What she wanted right now was, however spurious, a frothy sense of Christmas and not to be thinking of Angus. Fortnum & Mason, then! Everyone loved getting something from there. Maybe there would be pre-Christmas crowds, people happy to be shopping. Of course, she realized, part of the urgency of the crowds during the day was because they were all out getting what they could before they had to go down into the shelters again at night.

The windows of the Underground to Piccadilly Circus were clouded by the warm breath of cold riders. Lane cleared a little space with her fingers to look out into the darkness of the tunnel and thought about what she might buy. A new tablecloth? Definitely some lovely biscuits with chocolate on them. Her grandmother's letters had been full of good-humoured complaints about "poor" Alice who made dreadful biscuits, and dreadful everything else, for that matter, but who was nevertheless very sweet and did look after them well. Lovely chocolate biscuits would be most welcome. Perhaps a cookery book for poor Alice? She smiled at the foggy window, and then realized her stop was next. She'd hired Alice and had been impressed by her kindness and sweet temper. She had assumed she could cook, because she assumed that any girl not brought up with cooks and servants could cook. Apparently not. Well, Lane certainly couldn't talk. She was hopeless in the kitchen. She excused herself as she slid out past her well-bundled neighbour and alighted onto the Piccadilly platform. This was more like it! Crowds surged up the stairs and filled the street.

It felt almost normal to be jostled by people on the pavement. She walked past St. James and Hatchards bookshop, pausing under the irresistible urge to spend a happy half hour browsing among the books. She promised herself she'd stop after she'd bought her presents. The Fortnum & Mason windows looked more like their old selves with an over-cheerful Father Christmas on display . . . all right for him, she thought, and went in the door.

Inside Lane walked longingly past the cosmetic and handbag counters. It would be lovely to have a treat, even a new lipstick. But nothing, she told herself sternly, until she'd bought some proper presents. She made her way to household items and was just looking through the very posh Christmas tablecloths when she saw that they also sold old-fashioned Christmas tree candles. Perfect! She wasn't sure how available those would be in Broughton, but she knew that her grandparents had the brass holders, because she'd put them away herself onto a top shelf of the hall cupboard.

With candles in her shopping bag, she abandoned the tablecloth idea as too impersonal and found the confectionary counter downstairs, where she bought a box of chocolate biscuits. And then she pointed at a selection of chocolates under glass.

"Do you have one with an orange cream centre?"

"Certainly," the young woman with the white gloves said. "Would you like one?"

"Yes," said Lane, and feeling nearly reckless, she added, "let's make it six."

With her biscuits and chocolate paid for, she asked, "Which way to men's gloves?" On her way, she took a bite of a chocolate and had to stop and close her eyes. It was heavenly! She wondered why she didn't have chocolate more often. One could still get it, after all, and one little piece was hardly going to break the bank.

With a deep sigh, she popped the rest into her mouth

and found her way to men's furnishings. Some lovely warm gloves for Ganf, she thought, and perhaps a muffler for Grandmama? It was silly, that, because her grandmother was a prodigious knitter, and she was certain everyone in the village would have had a scarf from her by now. No. Something else. With gloves, biscuits, chocolates, and candles now in her bag, she wandered back to the cosmetics counters. She was stopped by a display at the perfume counter. Perfume? Yes! It was completely frivolous, and she was sure Grandmama would be pleased. She loved her little luxuries.

"For Grandmaman, the lilac is very nice," the young woman at the counter said in her French accent. "But a little expected, non?"

"Very expected," Lane said. Lilacs, violets, lavender, lily of the valley, all in the old-lady category. She thought of her grandmother in her youth, elegant and beautiful.

"Chanel No. 5. It is the most famous scent in the world."

"Yes," Lane said, without a moment's thought. There was a war on. When else ought one to spoil one's beloved grandmother with Chanel? "Chanel it is!"

"You have made a very good choice, mademoiselle," the young woman at the counter said. "And for yourself? A beautiful young woman like you is elevated by a wonderful scent—" She gave a gallic shrug. "— even in wartime. L'Heure Bleue, perhaps? Here, let me show you."

It was divine. Lane was terribly tempted. The scent brought back carefree times that it seemed might never come again. "I won't, thank you. But I think I will get some lipstick. Mine's nearly out."

"Here, a little spray to take you home this afternoon. Now, lipstick. Come over here with me to this counter. I will show you. Now for you, mademoiselle, I think a rich vibrant red, tending toward the colour of a sunset, no? Like this." She held up a gold case and wound the lipstick out. It was the kind of red Lane loved: a warm fiery red that told of tropical isles.

"Oh, gosh. It is nice." She gazed at it. Did she really need something as catchy as that? Where, after all, would she wear it? "Is this what they are wearing now in France, do you know?" She supposed the French must have an equivalent for "there's a war on, you know."

A lipstick like this might provide cover as well. She ought not jeopardize the "mission" by not committing completely to her cover.

"Of course." Then the shrug. "With the war everyone wants to pretend a little, do they not?"

"I certainly do," Lane said, very truthfully indeed. "I'll have that, please, and something younger, rose maybe, a gift for the maid." Poor Alice might as well have her little bit of luxury as well.

Hatchards, at last! Stepping into the shop felt as soothing as sliding into a hot bath. The smell of books, the incalculable wealth of hundreds of volumes on shelves, their spines calling out to her. New publications laid out temptingly on tables. Here, too, she had to shoulder past people. She looked at the new books on offer. Something distracting. Ngaio Marsh had something new, *Overture to Death*. She loved Marsh's crisp, slightly sardonic prose. Yes, that would keep her busy on the train. She was just making for the cash desk when her eye lit on something from Graham Greene: *The Confidential Agent*. She glanced at the back of the jacket and then put it firmly down. The title alone made it all feel too close to home. But there on a nearby table among the cookery books was a nice new edition of Mrs. Beeton. Should she? Would Alice think it an insult? She could buy it as a present for Grandmama, and then it wouldn't seem as if it were directed at Alice. Done. In any case, she reflected, sliding her books into her bag, there'd probably soon be nothing to cook at all if the war kept up, and the papers would be full of how to make cakes out of old newspaper or something.

In the crowded and steaming bus back to her neighbourhood, she wondered if she ought to read Mrs. Beeton instead of Miss Marsh. It would do her good.

"IRENE?" SHE CALLED out, as she pushed the door open. No answer. Lane breathed a sigh of relief. She didn't want to explain why she was suddenly dashing off to Scotland. She put her shopping down, pulled her suitcase out from under the bed, and then stopped. She pushed it back and frowned. She had shoved it under the bed with the back facing out. Had Irene been back and moved it? She quickly felt under the mattress and was relieved to find the revolver, ammunition, and map still there. She pulled them out and felt a surge of anxiety. She was sure she had folded the map properly. It looked slightly lumpy now, as if someone had folded it hurriedly.

No, she herself must have folded it like that, in a hurry to get out to her shopping. She shook her head at her own doubt. But her misgivings lingered. She suddenly wondered about Irene. Did she snoop in Lane's drawers or pockets? Did it mean anything if she did, or was it just that she was nosy? Lane remembered the hurried footsteps she'd heard at Barkley's door. This whole bloody mission was making her jumpy! She tried to brush away her new worry and think instead about what she might need. If she weren't going on this beastly mission, she would just be annoyed that Irene poked around in her things, but now she could feel a new anxiety about everything. She sighed. Packing, that's what she should be thinking about!

She would wear all her warm things, and pack undergarments, socks, and her green jumper and moss tweed skirt for an imagined Christmas Eve. She'd wear her wool trousers to travel in, and perhaps her wool-lined boots, and put a pair of pumps in the suitcase. Hairbrush, tooth things, cold cream, and last, the presents. There wasn't room for much more with those beastly snowshoes there! Where was her green jumper? She looked in her drawers and her side of the wardrobe. Nothing. Had she lent it to Irene? Feeling a tad guilty, she checked in Irene's side of the wardrobe and then went to her chest of drawers and pulled the top drawer open. It wasn't there, but it was in the second drawer. Irritated that Irene seemed to have nationalized her jumper, she took it out and was about to shut the drawer when she saw a piece of paper that had slid out from among the skirts as she moved them. She firmly began to shut the drawer but then stopped. It was a letter, in German. She threw her jumper on the bed and pulled it out, her heart pounding. Of course, Irene had said just today that she'd been there in her school days. This was bound to be a childhood chum. But she unfolded the paper anyway, unable to stop herself.

> *Darling Reiny,*
> *I fear there will be war, and I will lose all touch with you, my heart's heart. We must devise a way. It could be a little secret between us. The world could be crashing down around us, but we still, one on either side of the great gulf, will be able to talk to one another. Oh, how I long for this!*
> *Yours as ever,*
> *Franz.*

Lane looked at the date: March 1939. Before the start of the war. So, Irene had a beau in Germany. Was this the "fella" she said was in Africa? Lane glanced toward the door of the flat, and gingerly lifted the clothes up to see if there were any more. She realized it must have come out of the pocket of one of the skirts. Now in a quandary, she folded the letter and wondered where to put it back. Would Irene know Lane had been in her things? Too bad. She slid it back where she was sure it had been and closed the drawer.

Well, of course, it didn't matter. Hundreds of girls must have had boyfriends overseas before the war. She put her jumper to one side on her bed, clicked the bag open and tucked the jumper in, and then laid out the clothes she'd travel in. In her leather bag, she felt the steely resistance of the gun she'd pulled out from under the mattress. Her heart skipped a beat. She earnestly hoped she would never have to use it.

She pulled out the gun and looked at it. She was very well versed in its use. She'd gone often to the shooting club with her grandfather. But it was the one thing she dreaded, having to shoot someone. How would she behave if she was in a shoot-or-be-shot situation? Wasn't that what it came down to? Would one's instinct for survival take over? What about shoot or see someone else shot? That seemed a little clearer to her. She could imagine being able to kill someone who was threatening a child, or a member of one's team, or something.

She shuddered, checked it was loaded—it was—and slipped it back into her bag. With the gun and the ammunition, the bag was twice as heavy as it needed to be, she thought crossly. After a supper of toast and beans, she settled into her bed to read Ngaio Marsh.

She woke in the morning with a start. She got up and pulled the blackout curtains. It was dawn. She hadn't heard Irene come in, and was grateful that for once they'd not been ordered to the Underground. She dressed quickly and quietly and readied herself for the trip to the station, but then looked again where Irene's bed was, behind the curtain they'd fashioned. It was empty.

Where had she gone? She reminded herself that Irene was often away for the night. Perhaps one of the fellows she flirted so extravagantly with? It felt all of a piece, really, that Irene would treasure a letter from a former boyfriend. Still, a letter from a German at this juncture seemed at best ill-advised, at worst . . . at worst what? Suspect? No. She reminded herself not to be silly. Barking had put all this clandestine nonsense in her head.

Trying to suppress her anxiety, she positioned her wool tam on her head, wrapped a muffler around her neck, and then looked in the mirror and gave a nod. Why not? She took her new lipstick out of the bag, rejoicing in the weight of the brass case and the clean lines of the brand-new lipstick, and wound out just enough to apply it to her lips. Her face brightened up immediately, and she felt somewhat cheered. Right. She was off, and happy to get away before Irene came back. Just easier that way, she thought, but at the back of her mind she could see Irene rifling through her drawers, looking for . . . what?

CHAPTER FOUR

December 21, 1940

THE KNOCK ON THE DOOR startled them both. They were sitting in front of the fire with cups of tea, their feet encased in thick socks and slippers against the December cold and the snow that had seemed to be falling for all eternity. Poor Alice, as they called the girl from the village who did for them, had disappeared back to the kitchen after she'd left the tea tray and apparently hadn't heard the knocking.

Old Mr. Andrews—Ganf to everyone who knew him—hoisted himself out of the chair, happy to be abandoning the biscuit poor Alice had made of, as near as he could tell, gun oil and sawdust.

"Telegram, sir. Came in yesterday afternoon, but couldn't get up here with the storm. Sorry. Not bad news, I hope." The boy, under a snow-sprinkled cap and wreathed round with a thick wool muffler, had leaned his bicycle against the hedge at the bottom of the garden where the snow seemed bent on making it disappear. He was beaming up at Ganf, the brown envelope in his hand.

"Thank you, Arthur. I hope not, too." He reached into

a pocket and found a coin and handed it over. "I'd offer you a biscuit, but I'm afraid they're inedible."

Arthur, who sometimes rode their groceries up from the village in the basket of his bicycle, smiled and expertly flipped the coin. "That's alright, sir. This'll do nicely."

Ganf watched him kicking snow up with his boots as he went down the incline to the front gate, as if the weather had been provided entirely for his own enjoyment. Their cottage was on a gentle hill above the village, which today was obliterated by the snow. He closed the door and looked at the telegram.

The only people Ganf might worry about were his granddaughters, Lane and Diana, and Diana was safe as houses in South Africa, from where she sent dutiful monthly letters about how impossibly dull it was when everyone else in the world was having a lovely war and she was stuck so far away. Lane had been moved out of the range of the blitz after Wormwood Scrubs was bombed, and whatever outfit she was working for had had to relocate till the repairs were completed. He watched young Arthur cycling back down the hill, and thought with relief that it was a few more years before he'd be called up, anyway. It wasn't like the Great War where boys of fifteen were sneaking into the army. He hoped not, at least. With a sigh he rejoined his wife, anxious about the telegram.

"I hope this isn't bad news." He sliced the top of the envelope with his letter opener.

"I hope it's not about Stanton," Mrs. Andrews said anxiously. She was of the opinion that telegrams in wartime were bound to be bad. Stanton Winslow was the girls' father.

He'd been married to their beloved youngest daughter, who had died in '25. They knew he was a "courier," a euphemism for spy if there ever was one. She suspected his job was much more dangerous than he ever let on.

"It's from Lane!" he said happily. "'Marc and I will see you at Christmas. Stop.' Who the blazes is Marc?" He passed it into his wife's waiting hand, frowning.

"It's the best possible news, whoever he is. I didn't think anyone was getting time off at Christmas, with the war on. Oh, gosh. Poor Alice is going to be in charge of Christmas lunch! I wouldn't mind what she could cobble together for just us, but if our darling is going to be here . . ."

"And Marc," Ganf said, frowning. "Beau, do you think?"

"Surely not. But I don't care. It will be lovely to have someone here. We've been so used to big, glorious Christmases with lots of people around us." She fell silent, thinking of all those people they'd left behind in Latvia. Whatever had become of them all? And not just their friends in the English community. All their German friends had been ordered by Hitler to leave the only place they'd ever known. With Russians invading, Nazis encroaching, and terrible food shortages, Latvians had lost their country. She was grateful her husband's aunts had gone now, and did not have to endure all the terrible privations, or see their own homes taken from them.

As if he sensed where her mind had gone, Ganf patted her arm. "We'll have to find a good fat chicken. I shall make it my sole ambition." He looked at his pocket watch. "I've four days. I'll start with the MacPhersons up the hill at the farm. They might be willing to sell me one. We'll have to keep an eye on poor Alice . . . though roasting a chicken ought to be within anyone's capability, even hers."

"I'll get to work on the spare rooms, and let's make an effort to cheer the place up!" She drank the dregs of her tea happily and picked up the iron poker to give the fire a stab, sending up a stream of sparks as Ganf left the room. Then she sat back and looked around the little sitting room with its comfortable furniture and shelves of books. At least, she thought, we have this. We may be hungry for a decent roast beef and Yorkshire pudding, but we've comfortable furniture and plenty to read. She thought about the small wood of pine trees partway up the hill toward the next farm. The wind would have blown off some branches, and the cones would be scattered across the forest floor. That will be a start, she decided. At the sound of booted steps coming up the hall from the kitchen, she looked up to see Ganf in his waxed coat, his neck well wrapped in wool, umbrella in hand.

"Where do you think you're going in this weather?"

"I thought I'd get a start, see what the MacPhersons have available."

"Not in this you're not, with your chest. You can wait till it stops."

He stood looking disconsolate. "But I've just got all this lot on. It'll take hours to get it off again." He walked to the window and leaned over a little to peer up at the sky. "Ha! It's clearing up a bit. I'll give them your regards, shall I?"

She watched him down the path and out the gate. It was a hilly climb to the MacPhersons' farm. Perhaps it would do him good. Sighing, she realized that she'd not be able to put off her expedition on account of the snow, because he was right, it had nearly stopped.

"Alice!"

There was the sound of something metal falling over loudly, followed by an obscure Scots oath, and then Alice hurrying down the hall. "Yes, miss?"

"Is everything all right?"

Alice looked back. "Yes, miss. I just knocked the bed warmer off the hook."

"Good, if that's all. Well, get your galoshes on, and a thick, warm coat. We're going to the wood up the hill. Bring the bucket and a good knife."

"What are we going to do, miss?"

"Alice, dear, it's *missus*. We're going to collect some greenery to dress the place up a bit for Christmas."

"Will Mr. Andrews be coming?"

"No, he has gone off to reserve a chicken for Christmas from Mr. MacPherson. The turkeys have all gone to the war effort, apparently. Our granddaughter Lane will be coming with a friend to spend Christmas with us."

"That Miss Winslow that hired me, miss? Missus?"

"That's right. Now then, go get ready."

She herself was ready within five minutes and stood in the little foyer waiting for Alice. Honestly, she wondered, was Alice as dim as she sometimes seemed? Perhaps she ought to look at all the different ways in which people could be intelligent. It was wrong to be prejudiced about a girl just because she was an atrocious cook. She must have other virtues. She was very sweet. There was that. And quite pretty if you could overlook her perennial expression of surprise. As if everything that she encountered, however mundane, was quite new to her. Mrs. Andrews wondered if the girl read and might have been good at school. She had an admirer in the form of a lance corporal in a local regiment who had come around once to take her for a walk. Or had he been her brother?

At last Alice appeared, with bucket and knife, wearing a pair of black galoshes.

"Splendid. We won't cut anything off the trees, but there should be plenty on the ground after that last wind."

They set off up the hill, their breath coming out in clouds as they reached the forest. They struggled over a stile nearly buried in snow and began to walk slowly along the track that cut through the wood, looking about for windfall. The forest had been protected from the worst of the snowfall and the dark earth showed through in places.

"Look, miss, over there," Alice said suddenly.

"Well spotted, Alice!" Mrs. Andrews exclaimed. Ten feet off the path was a sizeable branch that had broken off a tall evergreen and would provide a good number of boughs. Alice set to work breaking the boughs off the branch, putting them carefully stem first into the bucket, and Mrs. Andrews went farther into the trees in pursuit of more boughs and some pinecones.

Though it was still only around three, the wood was a grey dark, as if night were falling earlier here than on the moor surrounding it. In the forest silence, Mrs. Andrews could hear the sound of herself breathing and of her own feet on the soft forest floor. She was filling her coat pockets with cones, and noting where they might get more boughs, when she suddenly realized how far away from Alice she'd gone.

She turned to go back and had walked not ten steps when she was arrested by the sight of something very unusual: a khaki shoulder bag. At least she thought it might be a shoulder bag. It was tangled on a branch and hung a little below head height. She stopped and looked around, fearful there might be a person, a dead airman perhaps, attached to the object, which certainly looked British. There was only a deep silence around her. She reached for the bag and then hesitated. Their son-in-law, Stanton, who was, after all, a spy, had instilled in them a natural caution. Indeed, the entire war had instilled such caution. The countryside was alive with rumours and fears about Nazis sneaking into the country and hiding among them.

Mrs. Andrews turned in the direction she thought she had left Alice and wondered if she would be able to find her way back to the bag with an official of some sort. The wireless had been warning them that people were sneaking in along the coast from Germany to spy, and even to scout in preparation for an invasion. What if this bag held a radio or weapons that had been dropped here by some fifth columnist to equip an alien spy? If that were the case, she ought not to leave it. What damage could be done in their village by some enemy alien who was even now somewhere preparing to find the things that had been lost when he parachuted into the country? Thus resolved, she wrestled the bag off the branch where it had become stuck and hoisted it over her head and across her shoulder, surprised at how light it was.

"Come, Alice. We're going back now," she said when she

found her way back to Alice, who had filled her bucket to overflowing with boughs and cones. "You've done splendidly. These will do nicely."

Alice, whose cheeks had become red from activity and the biting cold, nodded and said, "What have you got there, miss?"

"It's some sort of military bag. I'm going to take it to the authorities."

"Ooh! What's inside?"

"I haven't looked. Now let's just get home to a nice hot cup of tea. I'm a block of ice." They trudged back out into the deeper snow on the field. Just before they got to the path, Alice stopped, frowning.

"That wasn't us made that, miss." She was pointing to a disturbance in the snow about ten feet above where they stood. "Was it? We came in down there."

Clever Alice, thought Mrs. Andrews. She was right. They had come off the path and into the forest farther down the trail.

"Wait here," Mrs. Andrews instructed, putting the bag down in the snow. She made her way to the disturbance and stood looking at the footmarks. Boots going into the forest. She looked back toward the wood. Had someone been in there the whole time?

She hurried back as quickly as the snow would allow and took up the bag. "Come. Let's hurry back." Her heart was beating a little faster. It was probably nothing. Just a local farmer on the same mission as theirs. But they moved with as much speed as they could to the main path.

"Maybe it was Mr. Andrews on the way to the farm,"

suggested Alice, emitting puffs of cloud as she talked.

"I don't think so. He wouldn't go off the path, and anyway, those are quite fresh." Had whoever it was gone into the shadow of the wood just as they were coming out? she wondered.

It had begun to snow again in earnest, and Mrs. Andrews was thankful the path beneath the snow was rocky, which gave it a little traction. She began to imagine that whoever had gone into the forest might have heard them, discovered she had taken the bag, and might even now be in pursuit. She looked back nervously from time to time, though it was now nearly impossible to see the woods in the falling snow. Don't be a ninny! she thought. She'd been right in the first place. Whoever it was had just gone into the forest as they'd come out. If it was someone in search of the bag, they'd still be looking, but it was much more likely to be someone taking a shortcut through the forest to get to one of the farms on the other side.

They stumbled through the back door into the boot room and stopped, breathing heavily. Alice stomped on the floor to get the snow off her boots. She took off her tam and scarf and hung them on hooks, then reached over to take the bag and help Mrs. Andrews out of her coat and boots.

"I'll top up the kettle and we'll have tea in no time," Alice said. She kept an enormous kettle on the stove all day long.

Mrs. Andrews nodded gratefully. She took up the khaki bag and went through the kitchen and into the sitting room in her stocking feet. She threw another piece of wood on the fire and could hear Alice opening the stove and dropping more coal into it. She put the bag on the table, went to the door to get her slippers, and then sank into her chair to contemplate her find.

Should she look inside? What if the contents were booby-trapped? Or what if it belonged to a downed airman and they'd missed him in the woods? He might still be alive. It was too light to contain a radio. She was sure of this much. With alacrity, she rose from her chair and went to the telephone, which sat on a desk by the window, and rang through to the exchange.

"Where can I direct your call?"

Mrs. Andrews was momentarily stymied. She didn't know what military officials might be nearby. The Home Guard? "The police, please," she decided. Much the safest bet.

"Broughton police station, Constable Duncan speaking."

"Oh, good. Good afternoon, Constable Duncan, it's Mrs. Andrews up the hill at Two Oaks. I've just been in the woods collecting a few boughs and I've found something."

"In this weather, Mrs. Andrews? You ought not at your time of life."

"Really, Constable Duncan! Do you want to hear what I found or not?" He was a nice enough man, and no spring chicken himself, being too old to enlist, and certainly wouldn't win any prizes for intelligence.

"Yes, sorry."

"I found a khaki bag. An airman's bag, I think. It was caught on a tree, not like someone put it there, but as if it had been dropped. I'm worried there's an airman in the forest, perhaps still alive, who needs rescuing."

"Have you looked in the bag?"

"Just hold the phone," she said, and put the receiver on

its side on the table. She turned the bag the right side up and unlatched the two straps. But she didn't open it. She picked up the receiver again. "No," she said. "I thought I ought not to."

"Very wise," Duncan said.

CHAPTER FIVE

December 21, 1940

IT WAS DIABOLICAL, REALLY, AND just the sort of thing. She'd no sooner put her bag on the rack and sat down with her book when the door opened and someone came into the quiet compartment. Then, much to her surprise, the new someone cried, "Lane Winslow! I can't believe it! Isn't this just the end?"

Lane looked up and smiled. "Freda! What on earth are you doing here?" Her friend Freda Beauville was wearing a blue wool suit under her camel coat and a rather smart hat. Her very golden hair was rolled into a bun. She put her suitcase on the rack and dropped down opposite Lane, puffing as if she'd just been running to catch the train. She too, Lane noted, was wearing a rather dashing colour of red on her lips.

"Gosh, I haven't seen you since Oxford," Freda said, opening her bag and extracting a silver cigarette box. "Ciggy?" she offered.

Lane shook her head. "Where are you off to? Scotland, I assume, if you're on this train."

"Yes indeed. I'm escaping the blitz, just like you, I

imagine. I'm off to see my cousin just outside Edinburgh. She's invited me to spend the jolly old season not being bombed. What about you? You look like you're got up for some sort of Arctic expedition."

"I read about the weather. Perhaps I've overdone it. I'm off to spend Christmas with my grandparents."

Freda took a long drag on her cigarette and expelled smoke luxuriantly. "Gosh, I needed that. Now if we only had a little man to bring us a G and T like they do on Le Train Bleu, though I'd settle for straight gin about now. What have you been up to? Doing your bit, no doubt?"

"Very glamorous. Secretarial work. I was lucky to get a few days off. What about you?"

"All those languages you speak? Typing? Goodness, what a waste! I've been driving an ambulance. I got rather badly banged on the head a week or so ago when a bomb fell feet away from where I was driving and they've given me leave for a bit. I've put on my best suit and I'm getting the hell out of town."

Lane studied her. What did she see in Freda's eyes? Sadness? Anger? Perhaps the lovely hat, tilted forward on her forehead, covered up a wound, or something darker. "I'm sorry to hear that. The rest will do you good, then. Will you go back at it afterward?"

Freda shrugged. "I don't see how one can avoid it, do you? Herr Hitler isn't going to let up, is he? I've seen more than enough of mangled human flesh for a while." She took a deep breath and stubbed out her cigarette in a tiny portable ashtray she took from her sleek leather bag. "Well, I'm going to think of nothing but Christmas now.

My parents were most insistent that I go, so I am." Her cheerfulness sounded a little forced to Lane.

"It is remarkable that your parents let you sign on to the ambulance corps," Lane said. Freda came from a very upper-crust family.

"I insisted. They could hardly keep me in cotton wool in Knightsbridge, could they? It's rather time they learned that money can't buy everything."

Lane smiled. It had certainly bought that suit, she thought. She remembered Freda as she'd first met her, in a tutorial at her Oxford college. Freda had been reading literature, with a view to becoming a reviewer. She'd been quite brilliant as well as beautiful. Always fashionably dressed, her golden hair tucked behind one ear, a silver clip keeping it out of her eyes. It surprised her that Freda had chosen the ambulance corps. Women like her had been scooped up for much more glamorous work; Auxiliary Territorial Service or the Women's Royal Naval Service. Curious though she was, she wouldn't ask. It would only set off a conversation about war work, and she would rather steer well clear of having to make things up for the remainder of the trip.

"Remember Warton? I recall you got into a bit of a donnybrook with her over Sassoon," Lane said instead.

"Oh gosh, yes! Professor Warton. Honestly, what a stuffed shirt she was! We never did sign a peace accord, I'm afraid. I couldn't stick her hidebound views on war poetry, especially Sassoon. 'Too graphic,' she called it. Well, I'd love for her to come the rounds with me. She'd soon see 'graphic!'"

"It does sound like you're having a beastly time of it. I must say, I do wish myself back in the sunny quad of our college again."

"Oh, me too! It was such larks. One could forget about everything there and just live truly as one liked. I felt truly free for the first time. Did you feel that?"

Lane nodded. "I did, I think. Away from the expectations of my father and all that. But I suppose one just carries one's own self around after all, complete with all the parental expectations and disapproval tucked inside one's brain wherever one goes."

"Aren't you the cheery one! Listen, darling, I'm absolutely all in. This head injury, I think. It makes me frightfully sleepy, quite all of a sudden, and I didn't sleep a wink last night. You don't mind if I curl up for a little nap?" They were alone in their compartment and Freda leaned back against the window and stretched her legs out along the seat, her bespoke brown shoes just hanging off the edge.

"No, please. I've my book, so I'll be quite happy. I'll scoop you off the floor if you roll off."

"Done! And wake me if I'm still asleep by Edinburgh."

Lane settled into the corner of the seat, book in hand. She opened it to the first page, gently pressing the pages flat, but she looked out the window. They had finally cleared the suburbs and were into the country, picking up speed as they headed to the snowbound north. She glanced at Freda, who seemed already to be deeply asleep. They'd at least seven hours to go yet.

They passed a small suburban station, and out of habit, Lane looked to see the name, but then remembered that the boards had been taken down. She wondered where the ministry stashed all the road and railway signs. They'd been taken down all over the country to keep an invading army from finding its way anywhere. It would be like some sort of ancient time, she thought, when people just got around based on the shapes of buildings and landmarks. She wondered whether the lack of any identifying road signs would hamper her as well as the enemy. At least she had the map. With a sigh, she began to read.

Oxford, October 1938

THE SUN SHONE through the window, almost animating the dark furniture of her room. It had been raining for days, and Lane closed her eyes and turned her face toward the warmth. She had never imagined this particular kind of liberty: the freedom from expectation, and from the looming disapproval of her father and his stern mother. Just this, sunlight, distance, and a lovely couple of hours with the English literature tutor, the beginning of the Michaelmas term. Rumour had it that Professor Warton always performed her famed introduction to *Beowulf*, which included, if the gossip were true, a dramatic reading in original Old English.

With a start, she realized she'd be late if she didn't get a wiggle on. She seized her yellow cardigan, pushed her notebook and pencils into her bag, said a fond goodbye to her sunny view of the quad, and dashed out. Then dashed back in again, having forgotten her academic gown.

She was on time, but just. Professor Warton looked at

her with raised eyebrows from the large leather armchair from which she held court. "Miss Winslow, I expect?" she said by way of greeting.

"Good afternoon, Professor Warton." Lane looked wildly around for a place to settle. There were five chairs arrayed more or less in a semi-circle around the professor, and they were occupied by people who all wore the smug look of students who had arrived ten minutes early.

"Anywhere, Miss Winslow," said Warton, a touch impatiently.

"Yes, professor," Lane answered, and at that moment caught sight of a beautiful girl sitting on the window seat. The girl waved her over and shifted slightly, giving her room.

"Freda Beauville," the girl whispered.

"Lane Winslow," Lane whispered back, opening her bag.

Warton held up a book. "This is *Beowulf*. It is considered the beginning of the English canon of literature. That is by virtue of the fact that the text was written here in England, in a language we call Old English, which is itself a child of Scandinavian languages. These languages would ultimately struggle their way forward with Saxon through Old English, and then, with time, into Middle English, and so on until our current version of the language. But in some ways, it is not the beginning of the English canon at all—it's not even an English story. It tells a story that long predates the first invasion of Scandinavians to our shores. You can imagine them, arriving under the cover of darkness, on nights when the moon has waned, the sound of water lapping against their wooden ships, bringing with them the seeds of our destruction and the seeds of our transformation." She held the book up again. "And among the baggage they invade with is their old story, *Beowulf*. Here then, is that moment. I will read the first five pages as they were written."

"WELL!" LANE SAID when she and Freda were out on the quad.

"I know. She's quite brilliant the way she drops you right in it, isn't she? All that water lapping on moonless nights, people climbing aboard dear old Britannia with a sword in one hand and an epic in the other. I feel like I need a drink. Can I stand you a pint?"

"I'd love to, but I have to revise for a Russian exam."

Freda stopped and looked at her. "You speak Russian? You're a dark horse. Obviously, with that wonderful auburn hair. Next to it, blond is utterly clichéd, don't you think? What else do you speak? I can't speak anything!" She had pulled a lock of her own hair out to demonstrate its ordinariness, unsuccessfully, Lane thought. It was beautiful. She was not unlike the flaxen-haired beauties of Scandinavia. "French and German. Latvian. Alas, not Old English. *Beowulf* is going to be heavy going, I'm afraid."

Freda flapped her hand dismissively. "It was probably heavy going for the little chap that wrote it in the first place." Then she frowned. "Though she reads it like a native. Why do you have to revise for an exam at the beginning of the term? You haven't had a class yet, have you?"

"I think it's a sort of levelling business, so the professor can see how proficient we are."

Freda looked up momentarily with her eyes closed to catch the warmth of the sun and then pulled a silver cigarette case out of her bag and opened it, offering it to Lane. She shrugged when Lane demurred, pulled a cigarette out, tapped it on the case, and lit it with a silver lighter.

Lane had the idea Freda smoked to look sophisticated. She certainly looked graceful doing it. Lane's own father had smoked, and she had, as a consequence, never taken to it. Her grandmother had the idea that it was not only unladylike but unhealthy.

"Did you learn all that lot at your mother's knee or something?" Freda asked.

Lane shook her head. "Just an accident of upbringing. There's a big English community in Latvia, and I was born into it. I'm afraid it's nothing to do with any talent of my own. Where are you from?"

"Oh, you know," Freda said, exhaling a great cloud of smoke. "My people have a little sort of manor in Norfolk. There's a tiny village with a few forelock-tugging estate workers. Another cliché, I'm afraid. Daddy's on the continent a great deal and Mummy mopes about alternately feeling ill and giving lunches."

They had walked toward the gate and had stopped. The porter, Brinkman, was standing with his hands behind his back enjoying the afternoon. He glanced their way and nodded.

"I'm sorry to learn she's ill," Lane said.

"Oh, she's not really ill, I don't think. It's a sort of ennui. She fell into the trap so many women do: the promise of a good marriage to a wealthy and handsome man of her own class, only to find herself alone most of the time with a couple of children. She was frightfully useful during the Great War, you know, on the front line with bandages and bedpans. I suspect everything is really a bit of a bore compared to that." She dropped her barely smoked cigarette on the stone walkway and ground it with her shoe. "Then Daddy comes rolling home bringing a lot of guests and Mummy perks up like a plant getting a water at last. What about you?"

Lane considered. Her life, she reflected, was not much different, really, except her mother was dead. Her father was certainly away much of the time. "My sister and I were brought up by our grandparents. Very lovely people."

"You have a sister. Will she be coming up?"

Gosh, I hope not, thought Lane. Or at least, I hope I have my degree and am well away before then. "She's only fifteen. She's being educated at home. I shall be long gone by then."

"My brother, Brian, is a horror, but I'm quite fond of him. He's at Cambridge. You'll meet him. He'll certainly take to you!" She shook her head. "On second thought, we're unlikely to see hide nor hair. He's taking a commission and will be off to train to be some sort of aeroplane pilot."

"All this talk of war, I suppose," Lane said.

"It's frightful, isn't it? It makes me want that pint more than ever. Are you sure?"

"All right then, I expect my Russian will do."

"I wish I could speak something else. It would make me much more interesting." Freda sighed.

CHAPTER SIX

"**HAVE YOU LOOKED INSIDE?**" GANF asked, eyeing the khaki canvas bag as if it might explode. Outside, snow was coming down in thick flakes, mounding over the garden and settling so thickly along the edge that it crept up the corners of the window frames.

"I'm trying to think what Stanton would do," Mrs. Andrews answered.

"He'd be in there like a flash," Ganf said.

"Yes, but that's his job." In truth, Mrs. Andrews was in a quandary. She wanted to look inside more than life itself, but she thought it somehow might not be proper.

"Well, bully for him. I'm having a look." Ganf advanced on the bag where it lay on the table and stood for a few moments with his hands in his pockets, taking it in. "And I see you've already been at it. You really didn't open it?"

"I really didn't. It didn't seem quite nice."

"Nonsense! Anyway, you've been rattling the thing down the path and whatnot, and it hasn't exploded yet." He took his hands out of his pockets, gingerly lifted the flap, and began removing items one by one.

"Well, look at this. It's perfectly harmless, isn't it? A

hairbrush, playing cards, matches, a little chess set, a pencil, a toothbrush." There was a little brass vial with a screw-on lid. He held it near his ear and rattled it and heard one thing, like a small stone, banging around inside.

"All right, stop there," Mrs. Andrews said, taking the vial from him. "That is bound to be a cyanide pill. I've heard about those. They're so you can kill yourself before the enemy has a go. That means that nothing in there is innocent."

"Bar of soap," continued Ganf, "a change of underwear, a wool jumper, and . . . oh . . . a compass. Well, but that's nothing. I always travel with a compass. And these cards are English made, as are these—" He reached into the bottom of the bag. "—matches. Pearl Matches. Made right in London. This bag belongs to one of ours, which begs the question, where is he?"

The telephone rang. Mrs. Andrews picked up the earpiece and held the phone up to her mouth. "Broughton 31, Mrs. Andrews speaking."

Ganf watched as she glanced anxiously at the bag. He could hear only her end, and a muffled male voice coming down the line.

"Yes, I see. Right, then we'll do that. No, we think it's safe. Oh, I see, yes. Oh, good. Duncan, our local man. Good. Of course. Thank you, Sergeant. Yes, of course. How worrisome." She put the receiver back on its hook and rang off.

"That was someone from an airfield up near someplace called Drem. They can't send anyone because of the weather, all the vehicles that can travel in this are tied up, and could we look after it. They're worried it might belong to an airman who could have had trouble and parachuted to safety. They're going to send PC Duncan to look for anyone of that description with a few of the Home Guard. They've asked if I could show them where the bag was found. But, and I thought this very peculiar, they want us to hang on to the bag itself, put it safely somewhere, until they can get someone to it. Under no circumstances to give it to any of our local people, not even the authorities. They'll send someone along as soon as they can. Latest tomorrow morning. They seem to be worried about it falling into the wrong hands. I think it proves my point that nothing in there is innocent."

"Well, it may not be innocent, but it definitely belongs to one of ours, if they've a missing airman."

"Or someone pretending to be one of ours, and the Air Force chap didn't want to say," Mrs. Andrews said thoughtfully. "Let's put everything back and think about where to stash it." She turned and looked around the room, and then shook her head. "Not in here . . . too obvious."

Ganf, who was replacing the contents of the bag, stopped and looked at her. "Too obvious to whom? Will there be Nazis swarming all over the house looking for it? That seems highly unlikely."

Mrs. Andrews ignored him. "It could go into the blanket box in one of the spare rooms."

"Well, if you're talking about obvious, a blanket box fairly shouts, 'Look in me!' What about the airing cupboard? It has that low shelf we never put anything on. It goes quite far back."

She turned to look at him approvingly. "That is exactly

right. The airing cupboard. We can push it to the back where it will be quite invisible. Here, give it to me." She took the bag and very nearly hugged it. "This is too exciting!"

As Ganf was about to push the toothbrush back into the bag, he smiled and gave the brush head a little pull. To his amazement, it came loose readily and revealed itself to be the top of a thin, razor-sharp blade.

"Oh!" he cried. "Look at this!"

She was beside him instantly. "What did I tell you? Put that away at once! God knows what else is in there!"

"It does belong to a German spy!" Ganf exclaimed.

Mrs. Andrews shook her head. "No. We've been told whom it belongs to. Besides, it seems perfectly appropriate to me that a British airman might need something like that if he falls into enemy hands. Now let's get this thing out of the way before Alice finds it and has a rummage around in it!"

They had just secured the bag on the narrow bottom shelf, perhaps originally intended for drying shoes, when there was a knock on the door. They could hear Alice downstairs making her way down the passage from the kitchen, and then her voice sounding surprised. They arrived in the short hallway between the sitting room and the front door to find PC Duncan and two older men, all swaddled in hats and scarves and wearing heavy boots, pinned in the narrow hall by Alice, who didn't want them inside dripping on the floor.

"It's PC Duncan, miss, and Mr. McEachnie and Mr. Farris." Alice seemed reluctant to leave the crowded foyer in case one of the men escaped into the sitting room.

"Thank you, Alice, that's fine. Good afternoon, gentlemen.

Let me get into my things and I'll show you where I found the bag. Alice, could you bring my stick? I left it in the boot room. It might help with the slipping."

Ganf appeared in the doorway. "I'd better come along," he said with little enthusiasm, but then pulled himself together. A British airman might be lying wounded in the forest. He began to reach for his wool coat on the peg, but his wife stopped him.

"Someone has to be here in case there's a phone call." She turned to the men. "We're expecting our granddaughter to spend Christmas with us."

Alice appeared with the stick, and Mrs. Andrews said briskly, "Right. Off we go."

But PC Duncan didn't budge, and he was directly in front of the door. "We'll have the bag, if you please."

"I'm afraid not. I've strict instructions to keep it until someone can come down from the air base to pick it up." She was so firm that PC Duncan appeared unsure about his next move.

Finally, Mr. Farris said irritably, "Come on, Duncan. Get on your bike. The snow is going to bury whoever is out there if we don't find him fast." He pushed past the policeman and opened the door. "After you, Mrs. Andrews," he said, stepping to one side.

Alice and Ganf stood at the window watching them trudge down through the front garden and out the gate.

"She certainly seems to like tramping around outside in the snow. I can't see my gran doing that," Alice remarked.

Ganf chuckled. "She takes to snow like a fish to water. Never falls down, never loses her bearings. We're used to this."

"Gosh. We're not. It's usually raining here at this time of year. It's wet, like, but you can at least see where you're going."

"Well, they're all going to want something hot when they get back, so make sure there's a big kettle on the stove and—" He was going to say biscuits, but the recent ones had been so appalling, instead he said, "And do we have any of that Christmas cake left that Mrs. Elkin at the Grange made?"

"Oh, yes, sir. About a third of it. I was saving it for Christmas."

"Ah well, needs must. Get it ready for the returning party, there's a good girl."

THE SEARCH PARTY were breathing heavily, spouting steam into the air by the time they reached the edge of the wood. It would be fair to say that none of the men was prepared for the turn of speed Mrs. Andrews had shown, and they had had a job keeping up with her. She had moved another fifty feet into the forest before realizing they weren't right behind her.

"It's through here, gentlemen," she called out.

"Aye," muttered PC Duncan, and, taking a large desperate breath, following her. It was easier to walk in the wood, and they made good progress to where she'd found the bag.

"Here," she said, stopping. "It was hanging on that branch. I didn't think from looking at it that someone had deliberately put it there. The strap was quite tangled."

"Right," Farris said, "let's spread out from this point.

One in each direction. Thank you, Mrs. Andrews. You can go along home now."

"Certainly not. I'll go this way. May I suggest a whistle when one of us finds something?" She put her fingers up to her lips and blew a shrill and penetrating whistle to demonstrate, startling everyone. And with that she turned south to begin the search.

Duncan shook his head. "Well, you heard the woman. Let's get on with it."

In the end, it was he who found something. He was near the westside border of the trees when he spotted a patch of blood staining through the thin new fall of snow. He stooped to examine it. Animal? If so, there might be signs of the wounded animal going to ground somewhere, but whoever or whatever had been bleeding showed no signs of having moved. He walked to the outer edge of the trees, but there, the heavily falling snow had obliterated every landmark, bush, footstep, or path. He looked up at the trees adjacent to the stain. Slowly, as if his eyes were becoming accustomed to the anomalies, he saw that several branches had broken high above him in the circle formed by the four treetops directly above where he stood. Was that a parachute caught in the trees, or just more snow? Then he saw the ropes. He whistled as loudly as he could. He searched the ground for traces of the broken branches themselves, and eventually found one large branch lying five or so feet from where he stood, almost obscured by a layer of snow. He could understand why Mrs. Andrews hadn't seen it. It was a good distance from where she'd found the bag. The airman must have dropped the bag during his descent.

"What is it?" he heard Mr. Farris yelling.

"Parachute!" he called back.

Had a man fallen and cut himself free after being caught by the branches?

He called out, "Hello? Hello? Anyone here?" But the silence was absolute. He walked again to the edge of the wood to look out at the snowy expanse. He could hear the others coming toward where he stood. In the distance, he could see his friend Dillon's house looking as if it were a child's toy sinking into the pillowy drifts of snow. A tendril of smoke rose from the chimney. Could the fallen man have made his way there? He recalled Dillon wasn't on the telephone, so he wouldn't have been able to alert anyone. There would certainly be no tramping across that lot to get to the house. He knew one of the roads ran past the front of the farmhouse. They would have to get there on the road, if it was even passable. He doubted that; in fact, he doubted the road back to the village would be passable by this point.

After all Alice had done to make sure there was something for the returning search party, Duncan dashed everyone's hopes by not even going into the cottage after they had made the trudge back. "We'll have to get back and report what I found, and I'll try to get a vehicle up to Dillon's farm. If there's a, er, wounded man there, he won't have been able to notify us." And if there was a German there, he thought, Dillon might be in danger.

CHAPTER SEVEN

LANE HERSELF SLEPT BRIEFLY. THE steady rock of the train and the soothing prose of Ngaio Marsh overcame her, and she turned the book over and closed her eyes, feeling the luxury of sinking into sleep.

She jolted awake suddenly and looked around, frowning to see what might have woken her. Freda was still asleep across from her, and the train still chugged steadily along, its sound muffled by the snow. Then she caught sight of her book where it had slid onto the floor. She leaned over to pick it up and opened it to where she had stopped reading, the page falling open easily. She wondered what had woken her and felt a surge of anxiety about her mission, but everything in the carriage looked as it had when she'd drifted off, including Freda, sleeping gracefully across from her.

She gazed out the window, frowning at the beauty of the countryside sinking under its blanket of whiteness. It was the twenty-first of December, and it did not look like there would be any let up in the weather in two days' time. Her instructions had been to stay the night in Edinburgh at the White Hart, and then make her way to the coast. She was to catch a bus on the afternoon of the twenty-third to

Eyemouth, but the weather outside the train now would certainly not allow for much in the way of road traffic.

All right. No bus service, and maybe little other traffic. It was a trip that would only take a few hours in the summer. She was glad now of the extra day. The snowshoes had been a contingency. Walking that distance would take two very long days. It might take fifteen to twenty hours in good weather along the road. Given the snowshoes, was there a way she could go cross-country? She desperately wished she could take out her map, mindful of what Barkley had said about not showing anyone anything. For all it had been lovely to see Freda again, she once again earnestly wished herself alone in the compartment.

"GOSH, WHAT TIME is it?" Freda said, yawning. Lane looked up from her book to see Freda stretching and rubbing her eyes. She looked at her watch.

"Nearly five. You've had a good long sleep."

Freda swung her feet off the seat and pulled the curtain back a bit to look out the window. "Blimey. It's dark out. Shortest day of the year, isn't it? Look at that snow!" She stood up and stretched again. "I need a walk. I'll go in search of tea and something to eat, shall I?"

"That would be nice, actually. Here. Let me give you some money." Lane reached for her bag and found her change purse at the bottom, but before she'd opened it, Freda had her hand up.

"Good grief, no. You can stand the next one."

Lane watched Freda slide open the door and then slide it shut again, smiling at her through the glass and giving a little wave. How long would she be gone? Lane waited with a little flutter of anxiety, and then when it seemed Freda was not going to pop back in having forgotten something, she reached into her bag and took out her map.

She could see at once that if the snow was going to make travel difficult, she'd have a job on her hands. It wasn't far, as the crow flies, from Edinburgh to Eyemouth and just beyond to Armuth: just under fifty miles. She imagined a man arriving in the dark on the coast and finding no one to meet him. A stranger in a very strange land, every landmark obliterated by snow, every signpost obliterated by the government.

She might be able to traverse some of the distance with farmers who were braving the roads. The ordnance map showed the farms along the way. Perhaps she could do it in stages. This was a new and intriguing idea. Stay overnight at the White Hart, as instructed, and then use the next day to cover half the distance. She ran her fingers along the route, looking carefully at every marked building. She noted there was cluster of buildings a little past the halfway point that indicated some sort of hamlet. And there was a pub where she could spend the night.

She was just leaning in for a closer look when she heard footsteps. Controlling her desire to shove the map into her purse as it was, she folded it carefully with trembling hands, her heart in her mouth. She slid it into her bag, pulling out a handkerchief in as natural a manner as she could muster.

Freda was in the passage making faces at her, holding two cups and a bag in her mouth. Lane leaped up and pulled the compartment door open.

"Thank you, my dear. Now, congratulate me for getting two entire mugs of tea through two carriages without spilling any."

"Congratulations indeed!" Lane exclaimed. She'd taken the bag out of Freda's mouth and now took one of the mugs of tea.

"I put a shocking amount of sugar in the tea, I hope you don't mind. They had quite a big bowl of it . . . no food rationing on this train! I feel like we'll need it. I don't know how they still have any. The snow could strand us in the middle of nowhere and those three spoons of sugar will be the only thing keeping us alive through the long bitter winter."

"I love a shocking amount of sugar. What's in the bag?"

"Too thrilling! Bacon sandwiches! Now, what do you think of that?"

"I think it's a miracle," Lane said, genuinely. "I didn't realize how hungry I was." They were settled back into their seats, happily slurping tea and relishing their sandwiches.

Freda closed her eyes as she took a bite. "It's like we are in a never-never land. No war, no shortages, just us in this Christmas wonderland with bacon."

"It reminds me of the Christmas *piragi* our cook used to make. They're a sort of bacon bun with onions and raisins. It sounds a ghastly mixture, but it is the most delicious thing imaginable."

"Do you make them now that you're away from there?"

"Oh, God no. I don't make anything. I'm completely useless."

Freda smiled and drank her tea. "You'd better marry

well, then." She sighed. "I used to spend the summers with a friend by the sea, and her parents were quite ferocious. I don't know what Mother was thinking, really, sending me there. I suppose she just wanted to be rid of us. Anyway, the cook took pity on us and used to let us into the kitchen and showed us how to make a few things. If I'm ever stranded in a snowbank or something, I should be quite useful."

"Oh, good. That contingency does not seem as remote as it might at the moment," Lane said, smiling. But she saw something in Freda's expression that belied her light tone. It must, she thought, be a real nuisance to have such clear blue eyes. You would never be able to hide anything. Freda laughed off her family's neglect, but Lane suspected that she'd had a rather unhappy childhood. Well, Lane's own childhood had not been a trip to the seaside either, except for her grandparents. They had been her oasis. Thanks to their kindness, she had large swaths of childhood she could remember fondly.

"I have chocolate," she said. "I was at F and M getting a couple of little gifts and I bought a few chocolate orange creams."

"That," said Freda, "will more than make up for the bacon. I will be in your debt in perpetuity if you can place in my hand, right now, an orange cream chocolate!"

She took the chocolate Lane offered and bit off a corner. "Oh bliss!" she exclaimed. "To think I used to put the whole thing in my mouth and coldly eat through it as if it were not the most wonderful divine thing in the world! Now when I get a hold of something like this, I try to make it last as long as possible."

"I know what you mean. Will you be going straight to your aunt's house as soon as we arrive?"

"Yes. She's sending the car. Oh, it's such a shame we won't be spending more time together. I'd love for you to come to mine. But I suppose on these short holidays we must stick to our own."

Lane nodded and relished the elusive notion that she was on a holiday. With the diversion of the meal over, she began to worry again about the task before her. She thought about Freda, doing nothing more complex than driving an ambulance. Not a pleasant job by any means, but varied and actually helpful. Why had she not been signed up for that sort of war work? It would have been a good deal more exciting than what she did. Well, until now.

Oxford, October 1939

"THIS CAME FOR you, Miss Winslow." Brinkman reached into the mail cubicles and handed her an envelope. "From the president. Term's barely started. You in trouble already?"

Lane laughed. "I hope not. If I ever do get in trouble, I want it to be fun." She took the envelope to a bench and sat down. It was indeed from the president, requesting that Lane appear at her office at 2:15 that day. What now? She'd had a terse letter from her father telling her to stay in England and finish school and not to travel home to Riga under any circumstances. The political situation, he said, had become untenable. He was even at that moment arranging for her grandparents to remove from the country and settle in Britain for the duration.

"Dr. Oliphant," Lane said when she'd been ushered into the presence of the esteemed president of her college.

"Ah, yes. Miss Winslow. Sit down."

Lane sat nervously in the oak armchair before the president's desk.

"You've been here two years, is that right?" Dr. Oliphant peered at a sheet of paper that might, Lane thought, very well tell her that.

"Yes."

"Good. Finding everything to your liking?"

"Very much so, thank you, ma'am."

"Good. I'm afraid there will be a slight interruption in your career. We had an inquiry from the War Office, and you were mentioned in particular as perhaps being of interest. They were looking for students who speak French very well. I confirmed with them that you also speak German and Russian with equal facility. It would seem the war effort is in need of such abilities." She lifted her hand, as if Lane were about to object. "No, don't worry. Your place will still be here when it's over. I shouldn't think it will be more than a couple of years. No one, I hope, is mad enough to drag us into another long war. Sanity will prevail, I'm sure of it."

"What am I to do, Dr. Oliphant?" Lane's head whirled at this sudden intrusion of the war into her life and plans. The thing had only just started.

"You are to report to Major Barkley at Wormwood Scrubs in two days' time. You have leave to stop attending, and I recommend you go back to your rooms, pack, and get the morning train to town. You have people there?"

Lane nodded slowly. She did have an aunt in Kensington. She would have to write to her immediately, even knowing that she would likely turn up at the door before the letter arrived. She groaned inwardly. She'd spent several unhappy and lonely stays with her aunt as a child, and her ideas about children were positively medieval. Seen and not heard was her confirmed philosophy. She had no children of her own, but Lane did not doubt that if Aunt Elizabeth had had any, they'd have barely been seen and certainly never heard.

Lane had last visited her two years before during the season, as it was called, when she'd been brushed up and presented at court with the three obligatory Prince of Wales feathers in her hair. It was every deb's dream, but for Lane it had been a nightmare. The king had leaned forward and said something she'd been too nervous to hear. All she'd said was, "Your Majesty," and then she'd been shuffled along, red with humiliation. Her relief and joy at being told by her father she was to go immediately to Oxford at the end of the season was unconfined. She dreaded spending any time being dressed for display and going around looking for a suitable man. It was a positively archaic ritual, the whole thing.

"Miss Winslow?" The impatient tone of Dr. Oliphant's voice cut through her memories.

"Yes, I'm sorry," Lane said hurriedly.

"This is not a trivial call, Miss Winslow. We all must do our duty now. High and low alike are called. Do you understand?"

"Certainly, yes." Her words alarmed Lane. What was

all this "high and low" business? Did Dr. Oliphant think that being a member of the "high" she might opt to neglect her duty? Or did the president know something about the assignment? Surely, she was being called to translate. What else could she possibly be asked to do?

"That will be all, Miss Winslow. I wish you the very best."

Lane rose and thanked Dr. Oliphant and left her office in a daze. She had no inkling that this meeting was the very pivot upon which her life would turn forever.

CHAPTER EIGHT

"**Do you think the poor** man is still out there?" Alice asked. She and Mrs. Andrews were arranging the boughs they had brought from the forest along the window ledge and on the mantel. Ganf sat reading by the fire.

"Well, if he is, he'll be nothing but a mound of snow by now," Mrs. Andrews said. She'd been determined not to correct poor Alice's arrangement of the greenery, and she held her tongue now as Alice arranged a branch so the stem was the most visible element. Seeing that Alice was actually worried about the fate of a possible airman, she added, "I shouldn't worry, my dear. We didn't find him, so he has most certainly made his way to safety. Now then, I think I have a box of baubles and whatnot. Can you go into the spare room and fetch it from the top shelf of the wardrobe?"

"Yes, miss."

The minute she'd gone, Mrs. Andrews set about turning the boughs and tucking the stems in.

"I see what you're doing," Ganf said, looking over his glasses.

"It's maddening," she replied. "You'd think she'd never

arranged a bough in her life."

"Perhaps she hasn't. Perhaps her mother or older sisters did all that. She is the baby of the family, is she not?"

"Yes, of course. I'd quite forgotten. That would explain a great deal. It's already looking festive in here, don't you think?"

"Lane and Marc will be delighted, I'm sure. Will you be decorating right through teatime?"

"You think of nothing but your stomach," Mrs. Andrews said, though she'd have killed for a cup of tea herself.

"Do you think we could have some of that Christmas cake instead of those ghastly bis—"

"I've found it!" Alice exclaimed coming into the room. "There are some lovely things in here, and some very funny-looking old Father Christmases."

"Excellent. Thank you, Alice. Can you go through and make us all a pot of tea? I hadn't realized how late it is. I'll put these around."

"Certainly, miss. I'll bring the biscuits, too."

"By all means," said Mrs. Andrews, smiling wanly. At an anguished look from Ganf, she added, "Oh, and can we have a little of that Christmas cake? And bring three cups, my dear. We'll all sit here by the fire."

Quickly Mrs. Andrews distributed the baubles and stars about on the window ledge and the mantel. "Oh, look! Do you remember these? Our darling girl sent them when she was pregnant with Diana." She took out two Christmas cards, one with Father Christmas on a sleigh driven by a Russian coachman, and the second showing two Micky Mouse characters frolicking by a tree. She looked at them fondly for a moment and then held them up for Ganf to see.

He swallowed, nodded, and then wiped his hand across his eyes. "Our dear girl. She would be so proud to see the little ones now. Lane so clever and Diana so lively."

Mrs. Andrews placed the cards on either side of the greenery on the mantel and positioned the card they'd received from Lane in the middle. "I daresay that's one of the reasons Stanton is the way he is. He was very low when she died."

Ganf thought Stanton was very low before their beautiful daughter had died. She'd left two young girls, and she'd said desperately to him from her sick bed, "Don't let Stanton have them." Ganf did not want to burden his wife with his idea that Stanton Winslow had never been a kind or warm husband to their daughter. Much too driven by his work.

He shook off the guilt he felt about his views of his son-in-law, who had, after all, helped them to leave their old home and settle safely in this rather nice village in Scotland. "I'm sure that's the case. Ah! Here we are!" He put his paper aside and rubbed his hands together. Getting up, he moved the tea table forward and pulled a third chair so the three of them could enjoy the fire.

Alice put the tray down on the table and then stood uncertainly.

"Sit down, Alice dear. Not to worry. I'll be Mother."

The girl was about to sit when she saw the Christmas cards. "I didn't see them. They remind me of a card my mother has that she always keeps. What do they say? They've got funny writing on them."

"Just happy Christmas in Lettish," Mrs. Andrews said,

pouring milk into each cup. "Do sit down, dear."

The snow was unremitting. "The wireless says it's going to continue all night," Alice said. "I've never seen anything like it. My ma said there was a big blizzard in 1920-something. Usually when we get snow here, it goes away again in a minute."

"We are quite used to this," Ganf said, reaching for cake and eschewing the biscuits. "Remember last winter, my dear? It snowed like billy-o from December till the end of March at home, and didn't leave the ground till practically May." He stopped. *Home* was here now, he thought with a pang, missing all he'd ever known. "We're very used to this sort of snow."

His wife reached over and patted his hand. He took a small nibble of cake, perhaps fearing he might never get any again, and sighed happily. "Remember how we used to ski out into the countryside? I nearly got lost in a blizzard once with Heinrich Staller." He shook his head. "Poor devil. I wonder where he is now. We were such good friends."

"How could you be friends with a German?" blurted Alice.

"There wasn't a war then, my dear, and we all lived together on terms of the greatest respect and friendship," Ganf said.

"It doesn't seem right," Alice said, shuddering.

"No, I daresay in this day and age it isn't at all right," Mrs. Andrews said with a sigh. "But one day the war will be over, and we'll be on good terms with Germany again."

"I don't think so. Not ever. Have you heard how they're bombing London and Glasgow? I could never be friends with a German," Alice declared, shaking her head firmly.

She reached for a biscuit and then passed them by and went for a slice of cake. Ganf saw this and rolled his eyes, a movement his wife caught. She frowned at him.

"I have excellent news," Ganf announced suddenly. "That little trip I took to the MacPherson farm . . . I'd quite put it out of my mind with all this bag and missing airman business . . . we won't be getting a chicken. Instead, he will be preparing a goose for us! There, what do you think?"

"That is very good news," agreed Mrs. Andrews, though she cast a quick anxious glance at Alice, whose eyes had also lit up. "Do you think you could ask your mama how to cook it?"

"I'm sure I can," said Alice. "She will know. Will I be staying here?" She sounded a little wistful.

"Oh, I hadn't thought. Wouldn't you rather be at home with your family? Of course you would. Well then, you must ask your mother how to cook the thing, and then tell me, and I'll do it."

"Please, miss, I would rather stay here with you," Alice said, looking tentative. "I could go down to the village on Christmas Eve day, and then I can meet you at the church and come back with you."

"If that is truly what you'd like to do, of course," said Mrs. Andrews. "It will be jolly good fun. We can work out together how to make the lunch. If you're sure?"

"Thank you, miss. I'd like that."

"May I ask why you'd rather be here?" asked Ganf. He was very curious that a young woman of Alice's age would prefer to be away from her family.

Alice sighed. "Aye. You may. There are a lot of us, and I

have to share a room with my sister, and it's all noise and clamour. And I'm certain we will not be having anything so lovely as a goose."

"I tell you what, Alice. I will ask your mother if she would mind terribly much. I'll tell her we can't get on without you. How would that be?"

"Yes, please, miss. If you would."

"You are an astonishing adept at lying," Ganf said to his wife, when Alice was in the kitchen doing the washing up. "'Can't get on without her.' I expected a bolt of divine disapproval to strike you where you sat!"

"I did feel a touch of shame," Mrs. Andrews admitted. "But you know . . . I thought that perhaps, for whatever reason, she cannot get on without us."

FREDA LOOKED AT her watch and sighed. "We're an hour behind with this snow. My poor uncle will be there waiting for me."

"I'm sure he can get a cup of tea at the station," Lane said. She offered nothing about how she was to get to her grandparents' or anywhere else for that matter. "What does he do, your uncle?"

"He's a country solicitor. Quite smug and comfortable with the world." She looked vaguely disparaging as she said this. "He should see what we're having to do in London. He thinks Britain is the best of all possible worlds. He hasn't the least doubt that the Germans will be thwarted. Not the least."

Lane did not respond. Freda's doubt about the outcome of the war caught her off guard. Freda lifted her chin with a movement of some inner defiance and looked out the window into the darkness. "Well, look at what's going on! It would take a fool to imagine they can be stopped. We're all for it." For a moment, a chasm of despair seemed to open in Freda's voice.

Lane could feel her eyebrows coming together and stopped them. She was surprised by this dark turn in Freda's conversation. In some quarters, that sort of defeatism was very nearly treason.

"We shall have to try," Lane said, feeling rather at a loss for any other words.

"Yes, yes, of course we shall," Freda said, recovering and smiling ruefully at Lane. "I don't know what's got into me. Still a bit brought down by the bombing, I expect. We're terribly lucky to be getting out of it for a bit." She folded her hands on her lap in a kind of settling motion and said brightly, "Tell me more about what you have to eat at Christmas. It is absolutely my favourite subject at the moment!"

"It's funny, the thing I miss most are those little buns I told you about, *piragi*. And, of course, cake. My grandmother always supervised the making of the fruit cake. I miss the lead-up to Christmas. Everyone madly sending cards, the decorating. Cook making sugared orange peel for the cakes. And the lovely candles on the tree. It's like another world, really. Even after the Great War, everyone seems to have willfully ignored the possibility that there could ever be another war." Lane sighed.

"Gosh, candles! We've only ever used electric fairy lights. How romantic. My grandmother used candles, and someone had to be ready with a bucket in case the whole thing went up!"

"I found some candles in Fortnum's. My grandmother still has her holders for the tree. It'll be just my luck that she's come into the modern world and bought fairy lights."

The train began to slow, and the outskirts of Edinburgh passed outside the window, snowed under and still. "It's like a Christmas card, that," Freda said with a sigh. "Like a place captured in a moment of forever, with no hint of the war." She turned to Lane. "It's been so lovely seeing you, it really has. Like old times." She sounded wistful. And then she said, "Oh, Lane, do let's get together when we're back in town. I've really missed you."

Lane was surprised by the intense longing in Freda's words. She smiled. "Of course, we must. I'll call round at your parents', will I?"

Freda nodded. "Of course, yes." She stood, took down her bag and dropped it on the seat, and then pulled on her coat. "In the meantime, have a happy Christmas. Don't fret too much that you're not typing or whatever you do. It'll still be there when we get back to town!"

"I won't fret, believe me. You too. And happy Christmas."

Lane stood on the platform in the whirling snow watching Freda pull away. She had told her she was being picked up by someone from the village, and she did her best to look like someone impatiently waiting for a late ride. The minute the car Freda was in was swallowed in the snow and darkness, Lane turned and walked down toward the darkened street, hoping there might still be a cab. She'd memorized the part of the map she needed to get her to the inn near Portobello Beach in case there wasn't. It was nearly five, and in this snow, it might as well have been midnight. She didn't relish the long walk. With a genuine thanks to the heavens for small mercies, she saw one last lone cab waiting and hailed it.

CHAPTER NINE

"**HE IS ON HIS WAY,** sir."

The commandant winced. He had never been fully behind this effort to litter England with spies and fifth columnists. The invasion would not require it. It would be total. He sighed. Well, it wasn't his decision. He shifted on his chair uncomfortably because his hip hurt.

The bunker room smelled dank, of wet cement, and it was bloody cold.

"The place, it is remote? We usually go to the far north."

"It is farther south, a tiny cove, there will be no moon, the weather is bad. He will not be observed."

The commandant waved his arm as if brushing off a fly. "We have lost a number of men, drowned, shot, discovered. We cannot afford the drain on our manpower. You had better be sure."

"It is for this very reason I have contacted someone on that side to meet him. He expects to land alone like the others, to make his own way how he might. He will be pleased to be escorted by someone who knows the lie of the land and will get him out of the way of discovery the minute he lands."

The commandant frowned and looked closely at his underling. "You have contacted someone there? How can we trust him?"

"We can trust absolutely. The person is a dedicated apostle of the Fuhrer." His arm rose up automatically. "Heil Hitler. There are many who secretly wait for the invasion to bring order to their derelict country." He did not say it was a woman he had personally recruited and whose loyalty he had secured unequivocally. The commandant would not approve.

"When is he expected to land?"

"0100, sir, the twenty-fourth. He is already on board one of the U-16s. The landing site is extremely remote, and the weather currently is bad. The captain will signal our agent. No one will observe the landing. No one will expect one of our vessels this far south. The crew will then continue along up the coast to reconnoitre defenses and other potential landing spots."

"And if they are seen? If the British suspect and send someone to intercept him?"

"They will not, but if they meet any resistance from the locals, they will shoot to kill."

"WHAT BRINGS YOU to our neck of the woods, lovey?" asked Mrs. Harvey at the White Hart as Lane signed the register.

"You'll never believe it, but I've got a few days off and I'm going on a winter rambling holiday with a cousin. The train was late, so I'm stopping overnight here, and will meet her at our rendezvous tomorrow."

"Rambling! In this snow!" exclaimed Mrs. Harvey. "You

young people. We've got a war on, and you choose to march through deep snow like Trojans instead of putting your feet up when you get a minute to yourself! Well, I never." She reached behind her. "Here's your key, lovey, two floors up on the right. I hope you don't mind the two floors. I've an older gentleman below you who can't manage the stairs."

Changing into her brown wool skirt and green jumper, Lane stood just inside the door of the tiny room she'd been given and took a deep breath. She'd much rather have just gone to bed, but the plump and garrulous Mrs. Harvey had urged her to come down and have some supper. She'd a lovely warming potato and leek soup on offer, and she'd make sure Lane was at a little corner table right near the fire where she would be quite happy, and everyone was ever so friendly.

Lane went down the two narrow flights of stairs and made her way into the pub where a wall of noise and warmth hit her. Mrs. Harvey must have been watching for her because she slipped out from behind the bar and led her to the promised corner.

"It's never easy to travel alone as a young woman," she whispered to Lane. "Now, you sit yourself here, get warmed up, and I'll get your dinner out to you. I'll have Freddy bring you a pint of our best. What do you say to that?"

"It sounds absolutely lovely. I'm famished. You mustn't go to so much trouble," Lane protested. "I'll go get the pint."

"Nonsense. He'll be happy to do it. We don't usually get such handsome customers." She winked. "And from the south!" She winked again.

Lane smiled helplessly and settled in to look around

the room. The light was low and restful, and the room felt snug with the blackout curtains shutting out the world. It was very much a local. A pleasant hum of conversation was punctuated with the odd laugh. Everyone looked to be over fifty, and they were settled into corners and tables as if they were part of the furnishings. A couple of people across the room had stopped talking to look at her and, seeing her gaze sweep over, one of them lifted his tankard and nodded. Lane nodded back. If the intention was for her to blend in, it was certainly not going to be easy. She wondered when the place had last seen a Londoner.

She had just settled into eating the decidedly welcome potato soup when the door burst open and three uniformed men came in, stomping snow off their boots and laughing. Well, that answered her question. English airmen. She'd seen the nearby airfield on her map.

"Evening, landlord!" one of them called out into the sudden silence their appearance had caused.

The man who'd brought her beer nodded. Everyone watched as the three men found a cramped table near Lane. Two settled in, while one went to the bar. Slowly the conversations started up again, but they were desultory, as if the intrusion of the airmen had reminded them there was a war on outside this sanctuary, and the spirit of the evening deflated somehow. Lane had the feeling they'd been there often, and were not over welcome, in spite of the custom they brought.

"What's this?" One of the men at the table said suddenly, aiming this remark at her. "The scenery's not usually this good." He worked his way to her table and put a hand on it. "What can I get you, sweetheart?"

Before Lane could muster an answer, Mrs. Harvey was out from behind the bar, moving at a speed Lane wouldn't have credited her with.

"You can get her nothing," she said tersely to the airman, giving him a little push. She picked up Lane's soup and her pint and she said, "My daughter is back now, so we can bring these through to the parlour."

Lane stood, watching the rebuffed airman go up to the bar, laughing, and then followed Mrs. Harvey through a swinging door followed by cries of dismay from the other two airmen.

"They're a bloody nuisance, lovey. I mean, there's a war on, and they deserve our respect and all the rest of it, but they think every girl is their due. I can't stand it! Here, now. No one will bother you here." She set Lane's dinner on a table in what was clearly the Harvey's parlour. A cat curled by the coal stove looked up, and then closed its eyes and laid its head back down on the hearthrug.

"Thank you, Mrs. Harvey. Do you really have a daughter who's come back from somewhere?"

"No, love." She shook her head and sighed. "We had a daughter. She was a lovely girl. She died of the influenza. She was beautiful, like you." She lifted her shoulders as if pulling herself together. "Will you still try to meet your friends if it's like this tomorrow?"

"Oh, I am so sorry!" Lane exclaimed. Mrs. Harvey seemed resigned to the loss, so Lane moved on. "Yes, I think so. We said we'd be there no matter what. We have snowshoes. Are the telephones working?"

"So far. Snow this heavy can pull the lines down. Of course, if you're stuck here, we can all muck in together for Christmas. You'll be most welcome to stay. I'd best get back out, or those boys will be bothering someone else. They're just lads, really. Off on their own for the first time. High spirits."

"Very high," Lane agreed. "Thank you again. You've saved my day, you really have." Mrs. Harvey shook her head and smiled ruefully, and then bustled out the swinging door. Lane settled into the silence. When she could hear Mrs. Harvey's voice raised above the customers in the other room—"What'll it be, love?"—she settled into eating her soup, which was delicious, and smiled at the cat, grateful for the unlooked-for kindness of the landlady.

She wished she'd brought her map down, but she was certain there would be nothing driving on the road the next day if the snow kept up, so she'd be on her own. Fifty or so miles to cover by 0100 hours on December 24. Two days suddenly seemed hardly enough. That meant covering at least twenty miles the next day and then hoping the going would be easier on the second leg. She recalled seeing the name Meadowview Farm about ten miles along. It might be a stopping-off point where she could get a meal. Whatever it was, she'd still have as far again to go before that night if she was to cover a little under half the distance to Armuth tomorrow.

Her soup finished, she said a cheery goodnight to the cat and slipped through the door back to the bar. There were more people now, as if the snow had driven many not to their own homes but out to seek the warmth of the company of others. She could see Mrs. Harvey at the bar, and she stood at the end until she got the landlady's attention.

"Thank you, Mrs. Harvey. Can I settle up in the morning?"

"You do that, lovey. Breakfast at eight if you don't mind. We get an early start, especially now with the weather."

Smiling, Lane nodded. "Right you are. Goodnight then." But the landlady had already been pulled away by the press at the bar.

Upstairs, she checked the blackout curtains, turned on the bedside lamp, and pulled out her map. "Meadowview. Ah. Here we are," she muttered. Eleven miles, not ten. She sighed. In the summer, such a distance could be covered on foot in perhaps three hours, but in the snow, on snowshoes? If she could make it there by say 12:30 or 1:00, she could be at the hamlet she'd seen on the map by 4:00. It would already be very nearly dark.

She looked back at the map. Could she save time by cutting across country? Theoretically, yes, she decided. The road to Meadowview humped out for about two miles in a great northward curve. The farm was on the other side of that. It looked like she could save time by cutting across the curve. If there were no more snow. If it snowed overnight, the road would be still difficult to navigate, but the surrounding countryside might be almost impossible, what with fences, hedgerows, creeks, and gullies, all pitfalls hiding under their blanket of white. She guessed there would be very little traffic, with the possible exception of military vehicles, and maybe the odd intrepid farmer with draft horses or a tractor, which might be better equipped for the conditions.

If she had to dash about the countryside in snowshoes, it would have to be the road. An hour for every two miles? It would make for a very long day. She turned out the light, got up, and walked to the small window, moving the blackout curtains to look outside. The area was in complete darkness, a defence against German bombing. It was soothing to look at a true night, how the world looked before humans intruded with all their illumination.

Edinburgh, she knew, had largely been spared, the target for the bombs being mostly the industries of Glasgow, but even here they knew to their cost, they were never completely safe.

The snow had abated somewhat and left behind a blanket of pale reflective white. The road that ran past the inn was somewhat flattened by earlier traffic. If it didn't snow too much more, she might be able to do the trip in just her boots. She closed the curtain and prepared for bed in the dark, and then lay looking up into the blackness of the ceiling above her, the weight of her assignment suddenly looming large. What would her father think of her now? Perhaps he would think, as she herself was beginning to believe, that she was not cut out for this sort of thing. That she would fail. She turned on her side, pulling the blankets tightly around her body and closing her eyes. Something in her hardened. She'd jolly well prove him wrong.

"WELL, THAT'S TORN it," Ganf said. He'd risen early to listen to the wireless and was met with nothing but silence when he'd switched it on. He reached over and turned the switch on the lamp by his chair and it too was dead.

"Power's gone!" he shouted up the stairs. He stood by the window and sighed. Snow had finally stopped falling sometime in the night and the blankets of white undulated down the hill toward the village, where drifts of smoke from cottage chimneys rose into the morning.

Mrs. Andrews came into the room pulling her cardigan around her but looking cheerful. "It'll be quite like old times," she said. "Let's light the fire and then we'd better go get the lamps out of the shed. Did we lay in any kerosene?"

Ganf turned and shook his head. "Alice isn't going to like this. She's used to turning things on with a flip of a switch."

"Then it's a good thing we have a coal stove and a nice big pile of the stuff in the cellar. She won't be kept from cooking her world-class meals."

"Gosh. No power and an endless supply of Alice's cooking. We are lucky. I'll go get those lamps and make sure they're filled. Three do us?" Ganf asked.

"Bring four in case. I'm going in search of tea." She found Alice in the kitchen pouring water into the teapot and humming "Hark! The Herald," apparently unaware of the power crisis.

"Good morning, miss— missus," she said. "I'm just bringing along the tea, and the porridge is on the stove. The red currant today for your toast?"

"Good morning, Alice. Tea, splendid! Thank you, red currant will be admirable. We're having a little crisis. The power has gone down. It's all right for now, but we'll feel it in the evening. And of course, the wireless is off, and the telephone is bound to be as well."

"Oh," Alice said, as if she were not sure what to make of the news. "I wondered why I hadn't heard the wireless. Mister usually has it on first thing."

Mrs. Andrews smiled. The young, she thought, so blissfully ignorant of problems. She'd feel it, though, when it got dark and she couldn't read her ghastly novels. She followed Alice back to the dining room and watched while she set the tea things on the table in front of the window.

"It's lovely that, like on the Christmas cards," Alice said looking out at the snow. "It'll be a business getting down to the village. We should have skis or those snow things like those Canadian voyageurs I read about."

"Is the porridge all right, do you think?" Mrs. Andrews asked anxiously. She had no idea how long it had been on the stove.

"Oh, gosh!" Alice cried, and rushed out of the room.

Mrs. Andrews subsided into a chair and looked at the snow with a much more critical eye. It would be beastly getting around, and the possibility that the telephone would go worried her. Lane would surely be calling them to say when she'd be arriving, or if, God forbid, she couldn't arrive because of the weather. She got up and went to the desk to pick up the earpiece. There was a buzz. With relief she realized that it was still working—for now, anyway. She looked up as Ganf came in and sat in his place at the table. "The telephone's still working," she announced.

"The world could be going to perdition for all we know," he said. "Remember in the old days before the wireless, we had to wait days to find out what was going on? In the Great War, whatever news we got was days, or even weeks, old. By the time you read about something, it was over and done. You could right the world by just closing the paper and pottering out to the garden. Now it's an absolute barrage of constant news you can't do anything about."

"So, you aren't missing the wireless, then?" his wife said, pouring some milk into his cup.

"Of course I'm missing it! It's abominable. Ah."

It was Alice, a tray with two bowls of porridge in her hands. "I'm sorry. It's a little bit scorched. The stove is running a bit hotter than I expected. But with some cream and honey, you won't notice a thing."

"Perhaps, Alice, we wouldn't notice a thing if you didn't tell us about it," Ganf suggested.

"Never mind, dear. It looks perfect. Thank you. The honey is a lovely idea. When breakfast is over, we'll get everything ready for Christmas Eve. I don't think there's any hope of the power being back on." Seeing the expression of remorse on Alice's face, Mrs. Andrews added, "What about the toast?"

"Ah, well, no danger of that burning, since the toasting machine isn't working. I'll go do it on the stove." Relieved to be able to redeem herself after the burned porridge, Alice went off to the kitchen in a better frame of mind.

The jangling of the telephone made them all jump. Mrs. Andrews leaped up and went to answer. "Broughton 31, Mrs. Andrews speaking."

"This is Major Flint from the airbase."

"Yes, how do you do, Major Flint? Is everything all right? We've no power here, aside from the telephone."

"I'm sorry to hear that. Nothing wrong. Or perhaps

that's not quite true. I just wanted to let you know that we can't come and pick up the bag today, and it is vital that you keep it safe. Our vehicles are all tied up helping locals and keeping the critical roadways open for military traffic. This snow is unlike anything in recent years and it's coming at the worst possible time. Under no circumstances are you to give it to anyone who purports to be from the base. Is that clear?"

"Abundantly. May I ask what the danger is?"

There was a longish silence and then Flint cleared his throat. "We are now concerned that the man belonging to that bag is an enemy alien."

"But you said he might be British," she countered.

"Yes. Sorry about that. We don't like to raise the alarm, but I think now we have to. He seems to have vanished, and we cannot, at the moment, trace where he might have got to. That local constable of yours thought he might be at someone's house near the forest, and trekked all the way there, but nothing doing. I shouldn't be saying this to you, but best to prepare you. You will have to be on the alert. The trouble is, the Germans provide these blighters with our Air Force uniforms, so at first sight a civilian wouldn't recognize them."

CHAPTER TEN

Mrs. Andrews glanced at her husband, who was watching her with furrowed brow. "Are you sure?" She didn't like to say they'd been through the bag and found at least one apparently harmless personal effect was hiding a dagger.

"He may be innocent, but as I said, Germans are arriving here passing themselves off as English, so that bag may all be part of the act. The crucial thing is that no English airman has been reported missing, so we're certain he's German."

Mrs. Andrews nodded with a little thrill of triumph. That toothbrush dagger hadn't said "innocent" to her. Finally, she said, "May I ask, Major Flint, why I should trust you, for that matter? I do not know you from Adam, and you yourself could be the man you claim has gone missing."

The man on the other end of the line almost chuckled. "Admirable caution, Mrs. Andrews! I suggest you ask your exchange to put you through to Drem Airfield and ask for me, if this will reassure you. In the meantime, I beg of you to put that bag where no one can find it. It's quite safe there, as he won't know where it's got to. I don't know where the man has gone, but he's likely to cut his losses and move on to wherever he's going to rendezvous, so he probably won't go in search of that bag. If what you say is true, there's probably nothing critical in it he can't get somewhere here. But we will try to get to you by some time tomorrow."

LANE CONTEMPLATED HER suitcase. There would be no earthly use in packing a suitcase across the country. She would have to put everything she needed into her leather shoulder bag. Perhaps the landlady would let her stow her suitcase there. A plan had begun to take shape. She would get to Meadowview Farm, with any luck get something to eat, and try to cover the next ten miles in the afternoon. There was a farm listed as End House on her map. Perhaps she could sleep there. A similar program on the next day. She'd find a farm, she hoped, at the halfway mark for a brief rest. She'd do the last leg after dark, collect her party, and they would come back to the White Hart, and from here take the bus southwest to Broughton, assuming there would be buses running by then. It would be much easier than a hit-and-miss effort to get straight to Broughton from the pickup location.

Keeping the gun and torch within quick reach and her ordnance map folded into the right quadrant, she gathered a few necessaries, like a toothbrush and tooth powder, and packed them into her leather bag, and then re-packed the suitcase. With a sigh, she carefully stowed the Christmas presents she'd bought in the suitcase. If all went well, they'd still be delivered on the right day, she thought with slightly forced optimism. In a moment of rebellion, she took her little bag of three remaining chocolates and her new lipstick and dropped them into her shoulder bag. After all, who knew what would be awaiting her? One might as well look one's best and have something scrummy to eat.

Downstairs, she found Mrs. Harvey at the tiny front alcove from which she administered the activity of the inn.

"You're never going out in this?" Mrs. Harvey said in surprise, seeing Lane fully dressed for the out of doors.

"I'm afraid so! My rendezvous with my cousin was meant to be farther down the road at a farm. Here, let me settle up, and I wonder if I could ask the biggest favour? I wonder if you have a little corner back there where I could stash my suitcase. If I'm not able to meet my cousin where we agreed, I'll come back for it sooner, but otherwise our ramble is only meant to be a couple of days." She held up the suitcase apologetically.

"Of course," Mrs. Harvey said. "Of course. I have a little understairs cupboard right over there, lovey, do you see it? Nothing in there but dust. If you want, you can slip it in there. It'll be quite safe. Which farm are you off to?"

Ignoring the question, Lane said, "Thank you. That will do splendidly. It's only a couple of presents for my grandparents, not the Crown Jewels or anything."

"Lord alive, I hope you know what you're about," Mrs. Harvey said.

Lane smiled. "An adventure! If I don't catch a farmer on the road I have my trusty snowshoes. I'll be like Scott of the Antarctic!"

"Sooner you than me, dearie. Wait there. I'm going to get you a bun with some cheese to keep you going in case you get stuck. And a Thermos flask of tea. Not much sugar, I'm afraid."

Standing at the gate of the inn, sandwich and Thermos added to her bag, Lane looked at the narrow road. Certainly nothing had travelled on it that morning or overnight. But of course, it was Sunday. That meant, she realized, that there would be less traffic anyway, and she could escape curious questions about why she was tramping along the road on her own. On the other hand, any hope of cadging a ride was likely dashed as well.

The road running past the inn was covered in a fresh fall of snow and Lane tested it by walking a few yards in her boots. Her feet sank nearly five inches. It would be a hard slog to go ten miles in this, she thought, let alone twenty. Snowshoes it is, then! She leaned against the snowbank—which proved to be a snow-covered hedgerow at the side of the road which she sank into a little—and buckled them on. She'd practiced this upstairs in her room, but that had been sitting on the bed. She was glad they were a shorter version of the normal snowshoe. Eighteen inches was hardly tiny, but it would result in a much more natural gait than with the longer ones she'd seen.

She checked her watch. It was nearly nine. It had taken longer than she'd hoped. This little suburb of Edinburgh was eerily quiet. Smoke curling up from chimneys appeared to be the sum total of activity. With a quick adjustment of her muffler, hat, and bag across her shoulder, Lane set off down the road breathing at a steady pace, as if this were one of the cross-country ski trips of her youth. It took her some distance to get used to the gait, which required more leg lifting than ordinary walking, but the snowshoes were very effective in the fresh fall of snow. Could she cover two and a half miles every hour? That would get her there at about one.

After an hour, she stopped for a brief rest and ate several mouthfuls of snow to cool down. There had been thick grey cloud cover when she started, but now toward the east, she could see a slight patch of blue, which gave her a kind of specious hope. A post with no sign up ahead indicated an intersection. With a sigh, she set off again, trying to maintain her original pace. She was twenty yards from the intersection when she saw a horse emerge from the crossroad pulling a wagonload of wood. He had blinders and rocked his head from side to side in a steady rhythm with the effort of pulling his load, steam coming from his nostrils. Lane looked desperately at the bank of snow, which was no doubt a hedgerow, wondering if she should try to hide. As she was concluding that it wouldn't do to dive into a snowbank every time someone went by, the farmer, bundled up in wool, saw her, lifted his hand in greeting, and drove on through the intersection.

Lane waved back, sad to see him driving off in the wrong direction for her to hop on the back and catch a ride some of the distance she had to cover.

At the two-hour mark, Lane stopped to take a breath. Only one vehicle had passed her, going the other way toward town. A lorry labouring in the snow. The driver had been concentrating so hard he'd not seen her until the last moment, when she'd pressed herself against the snowy hedgerow to make room.

She reached into her bag for the sandwich. She'd eat half now. "God, that's good!" she announced to the silent snowy countryside. She pulled out the flask of tea and poured a small draught of it into the lid. Milky, sweeter than she thought it would be, hot. She closed her eyes in delight. Feeling considerably revived, she set off again. After another hour, she calculated she'd done the better part of six miles. She was hot and sweaty and had taken her muffler off, enjoying a blast of cold air on her neck. She resisted the temptation to remove her hat because she knew she would experience a rapid loss of heat.

There was a slightly raised embankment on this part of the road and she brushed snow aside to make herself a little seat. The map showed that she'd three miles to go. The entrance to the farm was around that large bend in the road, and then she'd have about 115 yards of roadway to the buildings. It was 12:05. She would have to get a move on to get there at 1:00 as she'd planned. She heaved herself up after a last swig of her tea and her remaining half sandwich, and set off at a good clip, her mind now on what might greet her there. A friendly farmer, she hoped. A dog that would not want to eviscerate her.

She began to turn her mind to the travel the next day, assuming she could get in another ten miles today. The rendezvous at Armuth was the next night. She wondered how she would cover the distance from this farm to the town by the next day, because conditions surely did not look like they'd be improving any time soon.

She had stepped up her pace in order to make her self-imposed deadline and, sweating and breathing gusts of steam into the air, she was relieved to see smoke as she rounded the last bend of the road. A few minutes farther and she saw the driveway to the farm. There was a sign that someone had partially brushed the snow off to reveal "adowview," and she gratefully turned off the road onto the driveway, where a set of footsteps showed that someone had been out that morning.

The farm consisted of a stone cottage and several outbuildings, including a timber barn of some size. She could hear the noise of cattle from inside, and a dog began to raise the alarm and ran out to meet her, barking in no friendly manner.

A shout from inside the barn told her the dog was called Bunch, and a middle-aged man emerged carrying a pail. He stared at her with undisguised suspicion. "What would you be wanting then?" he asked.

"Hello," Lane said. "I'm just on a trek to meet my cousin. I was hoping I could buy something to eat."

"You paying?"

"Yes, of course, and I have coupons," Lane said.

Still frowning, he indicated with jerk of his head that she should follow him. They walked around the barn and across to the kitchen entrance, where he stopped and looked at her feet.

"Right," she said, and bent to unbuckle the snowshoes. The buckles were caked with ice, and it was a struggle. Her legs felt oddly light in just her boots as she knocked the snow off the snowshoes and then stacked them against the wall by the door. Inside she found herself in a boot room, where she followed the farmer's example and took off her boots. In the kitchen, she was greeted by a slender woman with very fair hair almost tending to grey, who from her age she supposed to be the farmer's wife.

"I'm sorry to barge in on you like this. I just wondered if I could buy a little lunch and rest for a moment. I have money and my ration book. I'm supposed to be meeting my cousin in Armuth for a tramping holiday and I'm going to have to cover another ten miles today."

"I'm Mrs. Knox, dear. You must be hungry. Sit yourself down. Your name?"

"Lane Winslow," Lane said, sinking with enormous relief into a chair, and then wondering if the secrecy she was to maintain included not telling people her real name. "Oh, that's lovely!"

"Miss Winslow. Yes, that's all right then."

Her husband grunted, saying nothing, and went through into the passage, as if this had nothing to do with him.

"You'll be hungry. I've made made neeps and tatties with a little bacon and we've a little to share. Will that do ye?"

Lane wasn't clear what a neep was, but felt she could eat a chair if it were put before her. "It sounds like an absolute feast."

Mrs. Knox busied herself with a kettle and a teapot and Lane sank into the luxury of genuine physical tiredness. "It's so kind of you, Mrs. Knox."

"It's quite all right, Miss Winslow. I guess your holiday ramble has become a little more difficult with this snow."

Her husband returned and sat down opposite Lane. "I'll have my tea now," he said to his wife.

It was obvious he didn't want her there. She understood.

The news of the enemy sneaking into the country from isolated coastal locations made everyone jumpy. She saw a copy of *If the Invader Comes* tacked to the wall by the sink.

"You can have your vittles and move on."

"Danny!" his wife exclaimed.

"Enough, woman. I've said. You, have your tea and I'll take you out to the road. I don't hold with strangers, not when there's a war on."

Lane nodded. She ate quickly. Her urgency to be back on the road matched his to be rid of her.

CHAPTER ELEVEN

AS A SAFE STOP, IT left a lot to be desired, Lane thought, relieved to be trudging away from Meadowview Farm. She hadn't felt safe from the damn dog, and she certainly hadn't felt safe from the ill-tempered farmer. His wife, at least, had pushed a couple of thick slices of good brown bread and some chunks of cheese wrapped in brown paper into her rucksack quickly while the farmer had his back to them. She knew already she'd be panting to wolf them down before day's end. It was unbelievable how much energy it took to cover a long distance on snowshoes.

The light already suggested the coming long twilight of a winter afternoon. When she was well away and completely alone, she stopped to look at her map, and then sharply up at the sky. She had more than ten miles to go, and the sun would be down by four. Her heart quailed at the thought that she would have to make the most of those miles in the dark. As she shoved the map back into her rucksack, she encountered her Thermos and was ecstatic to find that the farmer's wife had filled it with something. Small mercies.

A deep breath, a whispered, "Off we go, my girl," and she took up her walk. She could already feel the drop in the temperature, so she moved more quickly, both to keep warm and to outrun the darkness. She reminded herself that snow was her natural métier, and tried to hum to herself, but her voice was stilled in her throat by the vast emptiness and silence of this abandoned countryside.

"I DON'T LIKE it," Ganf said in a low voice. "Not one bit." He was leaning toward his wife so he could speak more quietly. They didn't want to alarm Alice. "Who knew the place would be swarming with enemies? We might as well have stayed on the continent if we wanted to trip over Nazis every five feet."

Mrs. Andrews had taken up some knitting and was staring intently at it, but now she dropped it onto her lap and looked upward. "I think he ought to be stopped. We have his bag. What if he does find his way here? We'd have a perfect opportunity to nab him."

Ganf gnawed on the stem of his pipe. "Would we? Is it our job, I wonder? I suggest we wait for the chap from the Air Force to come fetch the bag and let them deal with it. Personally, I'm not that keen."

LANE FROWNED AND re-read her map. She had been planning to stop at Woodhill village. A pub had been indicated on her ordnance map a half mile through the village on the other side. She scowled at the sweeping snow and the increasingly darkening sky. It was still the better part of eight miles away. This was no time to hang about mulling it over. She had more than enough to worry about.

She folded the map and put it in the pocket of her

trousers, readjusted the rucksack, and set off at a pace she hoped to maintain with focus and the right kind of breathing. She would leave all thinking for later.

So meditative did her breathing become that she didn't hear the machine until it was right on top of her. She looked behind her and was amazed to see a small tractor pulling a flatbed carrying bales of hay only ten feet behind her. It puttered to a stop and rumbled noisily while the driver called out to her.

"You want a lift?"

Lane, still breathing heavily from her exertions, smiled and nodded, finally managing, "Yes, please! How far are you going?" Secrecy be damned!

"Hop up." He waved at the flatbed. He was at least fifty-five, Lane thought. A wiry man well-swaddled against the weather, with a voice only years of hard outdoor work and cigarettes could produce, nodded at her as if she'd said something he could agree with. "Off to a farm near Coldingham." He turned his head slightly to indicate the load on his flatbed, and then patted his steering wheel. "I've taken this lass out in worse'n this, and I thought I had the whole world to myself till I seen you. Where you off to in them things?"

"I'm supposed to meet a friend in Armuth for a winter ramble." Damn! She should have said her cousin. No harm done, but she'd have to be careful. Lane leaned over to unbuckle her snowshoes and throw them onto the trailer, and then clambered up after them, sitting right behind him. She was trying to remember how far Coldingham was from Armuth, but she was sure it was an awful lot closer than she was now. "Thank you so much. It's all a good deal more adventurous than I thought it would be!"

"English, eh?" He shook his head—as if confirming for himself that only an English girl would be daft enough to walk all over the countryside by herself in the dead of winter in the worst snow the north had seen in years—and slipped the tractor into gear. They bumped into motion.

Lane smiled ruefully. "That's right. I'm afraid I don't know this country that well." She had to speak loudly over the sound of the tractor.

"You don't say." Did he actually chortle?

"It all looked like such larks on the map back at home."

The farmer shook his head, and they travelled in silence for a good twenty minutes. Lane calculated what distance she might have covered on foot in that same twenty minutes and shook her own head. It seemed impossible suddenly that she could have imagined she'd make another eight miles in this, and then more than double that the following day. The sky was already greying toward darkness, and she closed her eyes and leaned back against a bale. They were going perhaps fifteen miles per hour, a lordly speed in her situation.

Lane leaned forward and called, "How far is Coldingham from Armuth?"

"Three, four miles."

She'd won the sweepstakes! Most of her distance covered on the first day! "Is there an inn there?"

"Aye. We're not likely to be there till seven."

"It's absolutely brilliant. Have you passed any traffic today?"

"Air Force lorry at an intersection. He had a job digging out a van that had got stuck and was blocking the road. Most intelligent folk are stayin' home to wait this out. This farmer needs his hay, though, and I promised I'd get it to him."

"She does very well in these conditions," Lane said, with genuine admiration, about the tractor.

He smiled and looked back at her for a moment to wink. "Better than you, lass!" He turned back to the road, and then said, "Fordson. My father got it in 1930, and it's been like a brick. Never any trouble in all those years. American. He saved up everything to get the damn thing. I didn't have new boots for years. But I got my reward. It's mine now."

Lane nodded. She wasn't sure if she had enough knowledge to carry on a long conversation about farming and was happy to note that after this last flurry of conversation, he was content to go back to his own thoughts—and a steady stream of cigarettes. Within an hour, the heat Lane had built up from walking had dissipated, leaving only a chilling sweat. She was sure the temperature was beginning to drop. She pulled her legs in close and wrapped her arms around them to make herself smaller and closed her eyes. The flatbed rocked slightly and the snowy ground they were covering softened its movement so that she dropped off to sleep, her cheek resting on her knee.

She woke with a start as the machine stopped. The farmer had turned off the engine and was hopping off the seat.

"Fuel," he said, and walked to the back of the flatbed, pushing through the soft piled snow with his heavy boots.

They appeared to be in the middle of nowhere and it

was quite dark. She looked at her watch in the dim light. Five-thirty already. She was stiff and cold. The farmer came back and opened the fuel cap, tipping a grey jerry can of something through its nozzle. It wasn't petrol, she was sure. Then she recognized the smell from the emergency lamps in her grandparents' cottage. Kerosene.

He put the can behind his seat on the trailer and went around the front to turn the crank. A couple of cranks and the engine rattled into life. "Already warmed up," he said. "It was the devil itself to start this morning. You normally need to feed the engine a little petrol to get it going."

"Where are we?" Lane shouted when they were underway again. Conversation required raised voices, with the tractor engine to fight.

"Got maybe an hour and a bit to go."

"That's brilliant," Lane said, and meant it, thinking of where she might have been, trudging far behind them somewhere on the road in the snow and dark. She suddenly remembered her rucksack. "I've got some bread and cheese and tea in my rucksack. Would you like some?" She'd give him the lid to drink out of and she'd drink it straight from the Thermos.

"Go on, then. Might as well keep ourselves entertained. It's not getting any warmer." Lane pulled out the brown paper parcel the kind wife had given her and found the two thick slices of cheese and two of bread. It smelled delicious and, now that she'd rested somewhat, all she could feel was hunger and the cold creeping through her boots. She put a slab of cheese on one of the hunks of bread and passed it forward to him.

They ate companionably for a while and then she said, "Tea?" He gave a nod and finished off his bread and cheese. Blessedly the tea was still reasonably hot, and steam rose as she filled the lid and passed it to him.

"I don't know how much sugar it has," she said. "The—" She nearly said, "The farmer's wife at Meadowview Farm," but there was Barkley in her head again reminding her not to tell anyone anything. "The landlady in Edinburgh was not generous with it at breakfast."

"Oh, aye. Well, this is good enough. Should see us through to Coldingham."

And it did. The village was in darkness, as if it had already turned in for the night, when he rumbled along the high street. He paused long enough for her to hop off with her rucksack, clutching her snowshoes awkwardly in her gloved hands.

"Inn over there," he said, pointing. "Good luck."

"Thank you so much for the ride. I'd never have got this far tramping around on my own. Oh, and happy Christmas." She stood, feeling a little regret at his going, and watched as the whole outfit turned along the curve of the street and disappeared into the night. In the silence, the village had the profound hush of a place abandoned.

I DO HAVE a room, as it happens. You from London?" The landlord, in his late forties, hair slicked back with brilliantine and sporting a toothbrush moustache, seemed intent on ingratiating himself. He had the register in front of him and turned it with a flourish so she could sign in. Lane nodded, and then wrote "Bella Rankin" on the line he'd pointed at.

"Bella, eh? You don't hear that name much anymore, do you? Nice old-fashioned sort of name. Where you off to in this weather?"

"Meeting my cousin at the coast." She was exhausted and still hadn't quite got over the cold of riding on the flatbed. What she'd like now was a hot bath and a deep sleep.

"Bathroom two doors down from yours. Give the boiler fifteen minutes. You'll get no more than a splash, I'm afraid. Toilet next to it. Food served till eight." He held up a key. "I hope you'll grace us with your presence."

Stilling a shudder as he engineered it so that his fingers touched hers at the handover of the key, she made her way upstairs and peered through the dimmest passage light imaginable at each of the doors until she found hers. Even the tiny room had the deeply embedded smell of tobacco, ale, and boiled meat that pervaded the rest of the establishment. But it also had a bed, onto which she collapsed, dropping her snowshoes and rucksack on the floor beside her. She could sort out her plans for the next day in the morning. Now she would go find some supper.

"I DON'T KNOW what's the matter with young people," the dowdy wife of the innkeeper said when she dished up some boiled potatoes with a surprising slice of gammon.

It wasn't much gammon, Lane noted, but it looked delicious and was, when all was said and done, bigger than anything she'd get in town with her ration book. In fact, between the previous inn and this one, she rather had a sense that food in rural regions was less scarce and controlled than it was in London. "Thank you. I'm starving and it looks delicious."

"Always dashing about," the woman complained. "There's a war on. You should be doing your bit, not gallivanting. You've not seen the signs, I suppose? 'Is this trip necessary?' I doubt yours is. And you can't be too careful. Don't know who's out there."

Lane sat directly under an enormous red "God Save the King" sign and was looking across at another one with a lurid red headline: "Beware of spies. Don't talk. The enemy has ears everywhere."

Yes, well, Lane thought. True enough. "Have you met other people gallivanting?"

"Another young girl a day ago. Headed out to the coast to visit a friend. For a week, she said! A whole week. Nice life. Looked able-bodied. I didn't take to her." She shook her head with disapproval and pursed her lips.

As she was firmly in the "guilty" column with this woman, Lane wasn't sure what to say, but she did feel a little relief that she wasn't the only young person out on a Christmas junket. It would, in a way, camouflage her.

"Yes. Of course. If it's any consolation, I'm only up for a couple of days. I'm due back at Christmas, you know, so family people can have a bit of time."

"Yes, well, I can't say I approve, but that is more like it. Eat up, my dear. You never know with the way things are if this will be your last meal."

With this cheery version of *bon appétit*, the woman went back to the bar. But Lane began to wonder about this gallivanting girl. Who was she? Surely taking to an expedition in this snow was unusual for anyone. Lane already thought the excuse she was given for her own mad expedition—a ramble with cousin—was paper thin and scarcely credible. Lane went to the bar and leaned forward, her hands on the rim. "I'm wondering if that girl is someone I know," she said, when she'd got the landlady's attention. "Do you remember her name? Or what she looks like?"

"Young, your age probably. Blond. She told me her name. Something ordinary. Anna, Ida, Mary, maybe. I don't know. I've got work to do."

"Can I look at the register? She stayed overnight, you said."

"Certainly not. That register is confidential. If she were a friend of yours, she'd have told you."

THE GENTLE RATTLE on her door handle startled her awake. She could not get her bearings at all. For a moment she couldn't even place where she was. Was it nearly morning? And then she remembered. Coldingham. Who the blazes was at the door? She cursed the blackout curtains and lay still.

There was the rattle again. "Come on, Bella love, le' me in."

With horror, she realized it was the landlord trying to get in. He was clearly drunk and slurring his words. No wonder his wife was so disagreeable! She had a momentary panic about whether she'd locked the door, and then wondered if he had another key. She could hear him breathing and hiccoughing, low down, as if he was trying to look in the keyhole.

He swore and then rattled the handle again. "I shaw the way you looked ad me." There was a long silence and then he tried the handle again. "That's not nice, ish it, love? See you in the morning. I'll be waiting." He started to walk away, and then his footsteps got louder as he came back. Suddenly he whispered loudly into the keyhole. "I know what you're doing. Treat me nice I won't call the authorities . . ." He seemed to run out of steam, but there were no receding footsteps.

She lay with the covers pulled up to her neck, her heart pounding. Finally, after what seemed an eternity, she heard footsteps retreating down the passage toward the stairs. When she was absolutely sure he was gone, she grabbed her watch off the bedside table and felt in her bag for her torch. Three in the morning! She ran to the window and pulled the curtain apart just enough to see onto the street below.

Compared to the utter darkness of the room, the street had the slight illumination from the snow. Nothing moved. She snapped the curtain shut, angry now. She wouldn't be able to wait till it was light. She'd have to leave now, hope he'd fallen into a drunken stupor so he wouldn't hear her. She took money from the purse in her rucksack and laid it on the dressing table, and then got ready to leave.

CHAPTER TWELVE

LANE WAS FURIOUS, AND RAVENOUS. Well, too bad. There'd be no breakfast. Nothing but snow till she'd got this man off his damn submarine. She resented having to go into the utter darkness at this time of night. She looked through the curtains. The high street was deep in snow and, if anything, darker than it had been when she'd gone to sleep. Then it occurred to her that it was better this way. She had some chance of making the final miles to Armuth, unobserved by anyone.

Well, here it was. It was December 23. Tonight was the night. She took momentary comfort that Armuth, if the farmer had been right, was four miles or less away. With luck she could get there before the populace really began to stir. Her big problem would be finding the cove once she was there. And finding a way to spend nearly twenty dreary hours in the cold until the submarine arrived.

If she could get to Eyemouth harbour, she could work her way south along the coast to the tiny hamlet of Armuth and the cove. She had counted the night before on the map. It was roughly the fourth cove down. Smaller than the previous three. At one in the morning, if the skies held clear, she should be able to see the dinghy come ashore. There would be almost no moon this night. A hindrance to getting around, but a help if one didn't want to be seen.

She slipped on her rucksack, opened her bedroom door, and listened. Silence. Praying that the stairs wouldn't squeak, she snuck down, keeping as close to the wall as possible. She was momentarily stymied by the door to the outside being locked, but then she saw it was a Yale lock, and carefully turned it until the door was free.

A cold wind snapped at her when she stepped onto the landing. She sat down and buckled on her snowshoes and made her way down the narrow street until she was clear of the last remaining buildings in the village. She realized she'd been hurrying and stopped to take a breath. She was at a crossroad. The posts for the signs were still standing, but like all the others, the signs were long gone. All the missing markers gave her an eerie sense of being in a world where everywhere was nowhere. She closed her eyes, took a calming breath, and remembered the map. In order to get to Eyemouth, she would have to go straight. The road was narrow and curved as it made for the coast, and for part of the way sunk between high hedgerows. If a vehicle came along, she'd have no place to get off the road. From there she would have to proceed south, maybe a mile or two along what looked on the map like a tiny lane.

She kept up a steady pace for two hours without meeting anyone. The grey line of dawn began to show along the horizon. That way was the sea. Whether it was the thought, or the reality, she began to smell salt on the air. She picked up the pace. Houses began to appear, at first scattered and then becoming denser. She had reached the outskirts of Eyemouth. She knew she must continue along this road that skirted the west side of the town, and then there would be a sharp turn left to the sea. She hoped the road to the port would be obvious.

The lane she was looking for, going south, was just before the water. Though it was still dark, she began to be alert for anyone out on the street. She could see the water in the distance, and then she noticed a low stone building with "Police" written over the door. She hurried past.

Though there had been a fresh fall of snow, the path had been trampled down the day before by busy townspeople. She could manage in her boots, and wouldn't leave a trail of snowshoe prints for anyone to find. A raised doorstep provided a seat, and with frozen fingers she pushed the icy residue of snow off the buckles and removed the snowshoes.

As she made her way down the street, her anxiety had begun to climb as she got closer to the object of the mission. What if she failed? If she did not find the man? What if she could not get him to her grandparents' cottage? What if she did find him and no one believed the cover story? They'd be arrested by the police or the local Air Raid Patrol, and she'd have no ability to explain. What if he came, and she missed him somehow and something awful happened to him? She closed her eyes in a wince.

She'd be shot out of her job and condemned to be a Land Girl for the rest of the war, weighed down with horrendous guilt over the fate of the double X spy her government wanted so badly.

"ARE YOU SURE you don't mind?" Mrs. Andrews held out the ration book as Alice finished winding the muffler around her neck and took up her basket.

"No, miss, missus. And I'll use some of my coupons for the extra butter and treacle. I'll stop and say hello to Mum, if that's all right."

"You do that, and give her my love. Then when you get home, we'll roll up our sleeves."

"Oh, I can't wait! Mum never let me help with the Christmas cake because I was too little. Only she always makes the cake in October, my mum." Alice looked a little puzzled.

"I know. It is the right time to make it, but I didn't expect we'd have anyone visiting this year, and I was a bit befuddled with all the new rationing. As soon as you get back, we'll get started."

Watching Alice clump down to the road to the village, she sighed. This was going to eat up a lot of coupons, but her optimism about teaching Alice to make a decent Christmas cake was unbounded. She turned around and looked into the cupboard. There were five little round containers of spices on the shelf from the previous tenants, and she took down the cinnamon, cloves, and ginger, opening each one and sniffing. She shrugged. They certainly weren't at their freshest, but at least the cloves still had some punch.

She threw another lump of coal into the stove and went back to the sitting room to look around at the decorations. They looked jolly festive, she decided, especially with the backdrop of snow through the windows. Good. Then she'd best get on with her knitting, if she was to be done by

Christmas Day.

She was quite asleep when Ganf came in from his walk and sat down disconsolately beside her in front of the fire, which was out.

"Nice walk?" Mrs. Andrews asked, pretending to have been awake all along.

"Where's the girl? I thought there might be some tea."

"She's gone to the village to fetch some supplies and see her mother." She looked up at the clock on the mantel. "She should be back any moment. I'm sure the water is hot on the hob. Tea is a good idea. I can fortify myself for the ordeal ahead." She put her knitting aside and stood, stretching with a little *oof* sound. "I'm sorry, I let the fire go out."

"Not to worry, I'll deal with it. You get the tea," Ganf said. "I still think it is ill-advised to involve her in this cake business."

"She's only a terrible cook because she's had no one to show her. She's very excited."

Ganf shook his head. Poor Alice excited about cooking must be the kiss of death for their cake. "Make sure you hide the sawdust!" he called after his wife as she disappeared down the hall.

"HERE IS THE recipe," Mrs. Andrews said to Alice. She had the *Wartime Kitchen* pamphlet open at the page. "But before we start anything, we must lay out all our ingredients and prepare the tin. Let's start with the tin. Get some brown paper and cut a circle the same size as the bottom." She walked Alice through all the steps, from cutting to greasing and fitting the paper into the tin. "Now then, fetch the big bowl and then we can lay everything we need out on the table."

Alice proved to be a most willing and eager student, and delighted in pouring treacle into the butter, reconstituted egg, and very small amount of sugar.

"Steady!" exclaimed her tutor, as she saw two months' ration of treacle cascading into the bowl. "All right, mix it well and we're going to add the flour and spices we mixed, along with a few tablespoons of tea. First the flour—stir gently!—then the tea, then more flour. That's the stuff! Now just wait here, I'm going to get something from the other room."

"You've never left her alone in there!" Ganf protested, when he saw his wife hurrying into the sitting room.

"Never mind that, give me your brandy."

"Not on your life!"

"Oh, don't be ridiculous!" Mrs. Andrews advanced on the cupboard where he kept his precious store of pre-war brandy. "We'll only use a tablespoon. We have to make up for the reconstituted powdered egg somehow." She took the bottle and went back to the kitchen.

"It's too bad we don't have an orange," she said, pulling off the cork. "We used to make lovely candied orange peel at home to put in the cake." She sighed, and then carefully poured brandy into her measuring spoon and capped it back up. "Good, mix that in carefully and then we're going to put in the sultanas."

"She's doing a wonderful job," she said to Ganf when she came back with his bottle. "You'd be amazed."

"I would indeed," he agreed, and went back to his paper.

She found Alice at the ready, spoon up, to put the sultanas in. "I saw my mother do this once. I think I can do it on my own."

"All right. Good, off you go then." She watched as Alice folded the sultanas into the batter and nodded approvingly. "Beautiful. Now, I want you to spoon half of that into the tin, and I'm going to get a silver sixpence to put in the cake, for luck. I have an old one that's still silver."

"Ooh, I hope I get it, I need some luck," Alice said, spooning the thick clumps of batter into the tin. "It's for George, really."

"Your young man? The one who takes you for walks?"

"Yes. Mum thinks I'm far too young. But she was married younger than me. She was seventeen!"

A whole year younger, Mrs. Andrews thought. She doubted that Alice would have a chance of marriage any time soon, with the war. Remembering only too well the blighted hopes of so many young girls in the last war, she went to the box she kept on the desk and took out a coin.

"Right. We'll wrap it tight in brown paper and pop it onto the batter, then shovel the rest of that on top. And scrape every last bit out of that bowl."

Alice obliged, and then looked at Mrs. Andrews. "Anything else?"

"Yes, indeed. Pick up the tin carefully about this high off the table and drop it. This takes out any air pockets. Then bung it in the oven and we wait a couple of hours."

Cake safely stowed, Alice smiled happily, running her spoon around the bowl and licking it. "It's good! My mother is going to be pleased with me! How did you learn? From your mother?"

"Good grief, no. My mother couldn't cook. Our cook at home let me help. It got me away from the governess, hiding out in the kitchens. We began every year in October with the candied peel. When that was done, we'd put the rest together. We made two or three enormous cakes . . . they'd take ages to bake. We had one for the family, and one for the servants, and one to cut up and take to a few of the poorer families." She sighed at the happy memory. Where had she heard that life was just made up of experiences you couldn't keep?

Alice seemed to sense her mood. "We've started a new tradition here, haven't we? You and I making the cake every year. Only next year we can start earlier. The war will be over by then, and we'll have everything we need! And I'll marry George, but I'll still work for you." She reached over and put her arm around Mrs. Andrews briefly.

"Yes, my dear," Mrs. Andrews said, much touched. "Yes, we have our new tradition indeed." But the war would not end, and one could only pray that her George would make it through.

CHAPTER THIRTEEN

THE MAN IN THE SHED shifted uncomfortably. He was sitting on a thin, worn horse blanket he'd found and was behind a pile of split wood. The cold was unbearable. He was furious. He'd landed far from where he was meant to be. He had watched the woman find the bag, had hidden on the hill to see where she went. He'd thought he could do without it, orient himself with what he'd committed to memory, but he'd lost an entire day trying to find where he was supposed to meet his contact. He needed that bag, and it was in this house, and now here he was, undecided about how to proceed.

It was fear, really, that held him back. He had his British airman's uniform on, but the trousers had been torn and the gash on his leg had stained them. He'd have a hard time covering that up. The only thing was to wait until they went to sleep and get inside to try to find it. There wasn't much time. The traitor would be landing after midnight. He shivered and shifted again. He'd have to make a move soon or he'd die of cold.

Suddenly the shed was filled with light. Someone was coming in with a lamp! He shrank against the wall, holding his breath. He could hear the lamp being put down and someone throwing wood into some sort of basket. He was whistling a Christmas song. "Stille Nacht." The intruder closed his eyes, as if this would keep him more hidden, and thought about the last time he'd cared about Christmas. Not for years. And yet the tune found a way to wind inside, unlocking some long-forgotten memory. Him, his sister, his mother. His father had been at the front, he remembered. He would never see him again, but that year they were full of optimism. He'd only been three. Well, he was twenty-six now, full of an English education, full of hatred for the people who'd killed his father and left his mother to fend for herself in a shattered country.

He reached into his pocket and pulled out his Luger, and then stood up. The man with the basket gasped and dropped it, spilling the wood onto the floor of the shed.

"Who the devil are you?" the old man asked. Apparently, he hadn't seen the weapon.

"Never mind who I am. Get into the house. No, no, leave that!"

"It's all very well for you to say leave it, but the fire's gone out and it's bloody cold inside. And stop waving that thing at me." The man sounded more irritated than afraid. The German prodded the Luger into the old man's midriff.

"Now, into the house," he said, and took up the lamp.

"What's your name, anyway?" The old man turned and was going out the shed door toward the kitchen door of the little cottage.

"It's not important. You have something of mine. I want it back."

"Darling, we have a visitor." Ganf appeared in the living room, the gun still poking into his back, the lamp swinging in the visitor's hand and casting a bizarre symphony of light and shadow on the walls.

"He says we have something of his," Ganf said, his hands up.

Mrs. Andrews looked at the man. She hadn't seen the gun yet. "You'd better sit down. Did you get the firewood, darling?"

"No. This gentleman seemed to be against it."

"What is your name? I'm Mrs. Andrews. This is Mister."

"It's really none of your business," the man repeated, in a perfect English accent.

"You speak English very well," she said, a little surprised. She'd noticed his torn, bloodstained trouser leg.

"Cambridge," he said. "Where's my bag?"

"I'm afraid I can't give that to you. I've instructions, you see."

The man put his arm around Ganf's neck suddenly and held the gun to his temple. "Mine are the only instructions that matter. My bag." His voice was hard and low.

"I see." Mrs. Andrews got up slowly and moved toward the low bank of cupboards along the front window. This would keep him looking forward, keep his back to the hall. Ganf was making choking noises. "It's in here somewhere," she said, trying to keep the tremble out of her voice. "Could you loosen your grip on my husband's neck? His heart isn't what it was."

She turned back to look at them, to make sure about what she'd seen. "Please." Ganf had gone a very funny colour. To her enormous relief, the man let up slightly on his stranglehold, and Ganf coughed and spluttered, sucking in air.

Turning back to the cupboard, Mrs. Andrews kept up a steady stream of talk. "I put it in here, so it would be close to the door when they came to get it. A man from the Air Force said someone like you might come, and that we should make sure to only give it to a proper member of the Air Force."

"Shut—" said the German, and then there was a thud, and he crumpled to the floor.

Ganf, suddenly freed, whirled around and saw Alice wide-eyed and holding a heavy frying pan.

"Good girl!" he cried, followed by a coughing spasm.

"My poor Ganf, are you all right?" Mrs. Andrews, the fear and relief overtaking her all at once, was by his side, holding one hand to his cheek.

"Perfectly, my dear," he said, coughing again. He had his hand to his neck, but then pointed at Alice. "Did you see this? What a splendid girl!"

"I confess, I saw her tiptoeing down the passage. I wasn't sure what to expect, but this is a very good result." She looked down at the interloper, who began to groan. "I shouldn't worry," she said to Alice, who was now looking down in horror at her handiwork. "You've not killed him. But we'd better tie him up and call someone. Alice, dear, can you go fetch the clothesline rope? It should do for this. And could you make it quick as you like?" She didn't like that the man appeared to be stirring slightly. She wanted to avoid any further clonking on the head.

Alice ran to the kitchen, and in a jiffy was back with a

length of thin but sturdy cotton rope.

"Allow me," said Ganf, who had recovered most of his aplomb. "Stanton taught me how to do this one afternoon a couple of years ago." He sat the groaning man up, not an easy feat. "Here, hold him up, would you two?" With the two women each holding a shoulder to keep the man seated, Ganf pulled his hands behind his back and began to loop the rope in a figure eight between his hands, securing the rope at his wrists. "Let's move him to the wall so he can sit against it. He's quite cold. Alice, can you get a blanket from the spare room?"

Mrs. Andrews and Ganf collapsed in their chairs and looked at their prisoner, whom they'd propped up beside the fireplace. "What does it say we should do at this juncture in the *What to Do If Invaded* pamphlet?" Ganf asked.

Mrs. Andrews got up, went to the desk, began to read, and then looked up. "It says we should determine if he is one of ours or simply dressed up to look like one of ours, and to use our common sense."

Ganf frowned and shook his head. "Don't think he's one of ours. And that is definitely not one of ours." He nodded toward the Luger lying on the floor where their guest had dropped it. With a sigh, he too got up, picked up the weapon, and looked around for a place to put it. He decided on the top drawer of the desk. "I'd better go out and get that wood and get this fire going. That's the first bit of common sense."

Alice had returned with the blanket. Mrs. Andrews laid it over the man, whose head lolled forward, and tucked it around his shoulders. "You'd better see to some tea, and the cake! I'd quite forgotten. Do you know how to test if a cake is done?"

"Oh," Alice said, unable to take her eyes off the man on the floor. "No, I don't think I do."

"Get a clean piece of straw from the broom and open the oven and put the straw into the middle of the cake. If it comes out with no wet dough on it, the cake is ready. All right?"

Alice nodded rapidly and walked backward toward the hallway, still looking at the man, before finally turning and hurrying to the kitchen.

The man made another sound and tried to hold up his head. "*Wo* . . ." he said weakly, and then opened his eyes and tried to focus on the room.

Mrs. Andrews said, "You are here, in Scotland. You tried to hold us up with your gun. I'm going to just look at your head, if I may?" She stooped down and gently felt the back of his head. "You have quite a bump there, but you should be all right in time. I see you have a nasty gash on your leg as well. You must have got that when you landed with your parachute in the wood. I'll put something on that. We don't want it getting infected. The girl is just getting some tea, and I'll try to get some into you. We'll build up the fire, now that my husband is able to go and fetch the wood without your interference. Are you warm enough?"

"Go to the devil!"

She shrugged. "I understand how you feel. You won't have to stay here long. I'll call for help."

The man leaned back against the wall, and then winced where the lump on his head touched it. Mrs. Andrews got up and found the number for the Air Force base. It would be dark soon and the power was still out. "Yes, Major Flint, please."

There was a long pause while Ganf came back and put some wood and twisted-up newspaper into the fireplace and set it alight.

"Yes, Major Flint. I'm glad I caught you. I think we have your missing German. At least, I hope so, or we've done something dreadful to one of our own." She explained briefly and then waited for instructions. "Oh, yes. Quite sure. My husband knows about knots. Right you are." She rang off just as Alice came through with the tea things.

"It's like this," Alice said, holding up the broom straw. It had nothing clinging to it but a couple of crumbs, but she was looking down nervously at the German.

"Perfect. Get it out and put it on a rack, and let's leave it there for half an hour before we take it out of the tin."

"It smells really good," Alice said, and then glared at the prisoner. "He's not getting any!"

"Now, Alice, we mustn't be ungenerous at this time of year." Mrs. Andrews only half meant it.

"There is nowhere that says we have to feed the enemy cake!" Alice said, and went haughtily back to the kitchen. She'd clearly recovered from attacking the man with her frying pan.

The prisoner was not, it turned out, too proud to drink the tea that Mrs. Andrews offered him. She had Alice make him a piece of toast with jam, which she fed him between sips.

"What are you doing here?" she asked, conversationally. "I mean, I imagine you've come to spy on the coastal defences, but I'm surprised you've not brought a radio. Then you must be expecting to meet someone already here."

The prisoner closed his eyes and didn't answer. She hadn't imagined he would. At the sound of the telephone bell, Mrs. Andrews practically leaped to the desk and seized the machine.

She dispensed with the usual formalities. "Yes?"

Crestfallen, she listened to the voice at the other end. "I see. Yes."

She rang off and turned back to the others. "I'm afraid you will be our guest overnight," she said. "One of the Jeeps has broken down and they can't spare the other, as it's on another assignment. We won't mind. We've enough supper, and we can make you comfortable here by the fire with a blanket."

THANKFUL FOR THE map, which she had tried memorize so that she might look less like a suspicious stranger, Lane made her way toward the harbour. At that hour, she was sure she would see no one in the street. But as she rounded a bend down toward the water, she saw two men coming up the road toward her. They were some hundred yards away, carrying torches and chatting. Home Guard! She could just make out the telltale armband on one of their coats.

She cursed under her breath and began to back up the street until she reached an intersection of a lane so tiny she hadn't noticed it in the dark. If she went to the right, she might hide in the shadows until they passed.

Blast! Her footsteps would surely give her away.

"Talk to no one." Barkley's orders rang in her ear. If

the Home Guard found her, a stranger walking around at this time of morning, they would most certainly detain her and interrogate her, and she wouldn't make the meeting in the cove. Then a childhood game of hide and seek she'd played with the gardener came to her. She hurried across the road to the other side of the lane and walked about ten paces, and then without turning walked backward, stepping in her own footsteps. At the street, her breath coming in nervous gasps, she looked for the men. They had come maybe half the distance and had stopped. They were shining their torches right and left up another tiny street. Still walking backward, she covered the distance to the other side of the road in an instant, and then continued backward up the lane.

She hadn't quite made it to the cover of the hedge when she saw the torches swinging their light across the intersection. She could hear one of the men exclaiming and she threw herself face down into the snow scarcely daring to breathe, cursing the efficiency and dedication of the Home Guard. In the dark they might not see her, and their torch light might not come this far. She prayed it would be so.

They had definitely stopped.

"Someone's been here. Those are fresh prints," one of the men said in a low gravelly voice.

"Hoy!" the second one called out in something between a loud whisper and a low call. "Show yourself!"

"Look. Whoever it was went up there. I expect it was Rick. He lives up that way."

"What's he doin' up at this time?"

"Gettin' away from his missus, I shouldn't wonder. Come on. I told Sal to have the kettle on."

"I don't know. I told you, I seen lights out on the water two nights ago. You mark my words . . ."

The voices faded as the men went away from her up the street in the opposite direction. She exhaled. Her deception had worked. Feeling blissfully hidden in the dark, she jumped up and stumbled as quickly as she was able along the hedgerow until she was in the wood. Here she stopped and bent over to catch her breath.

She calculated she was a little south of the harbour now. She tried to bring her map to mind. This was not the path she'd been aiming for, but she knew there was a narrow lane that dwindled into a footpath making toward Armuth. Was this it? She had, if she could stay away from the assiduous men guarding this little town, nothing but time. She had to head south of the harbour in any case, so rather than risk going back onto the street, she decided to follow this lane.

She was on the outer perimeter of the village where homes gave way gradually to fields. She passed two houses set a good way back from what had now become a path at the bottom of long gardens, and then came to a two-step stile into a fenced field. A slight indent running along the edge of the field told her it was likely the public footpath, and she looked for a sign with the name. But of course, she encountered only an empty signpost.

She climbed the stile and walked for some time at the edge of the field, its few remaining stalks of barley sticking through the blanket of snow. It would be properly morning soon and she wanted to find the large wooded area her map had shown her, to wait out the day.

Now well away from the town, the path had become a narrow track very nearly obscured by the snow, but for the fact that it had been recently used by another intrepid walker, quite evidently with a dog. She wondered if she ought to put the blasted snowshoes back on. The snow, now up to her ankles, was slowing her down. Stopping, she looked nervously around to see if anyone had ventured onto the field, and then took off her rucksack, unfastened the snowshoes, and buckled them on. She had to remove her gloves, and her fingers were quickly rendered nearly useless by the cold and snow.

Growling about the whole procedure and heartily tired of the snowshoes, she made her way to the end of the field, took herself and the snowshoes awkwardly through the kissing gate into the next one, and at once found that the path was taking her away from the water. She stopped to consider, and then noted a wood forty yards up ahead on the seaward side of the path. She would have to wait out in the cold for the entire day and a good deal of the night. Might as well do it in the cover of the wood. She could spend part of the day trying to find the right rendezvous place, and then sit down somewhere to rest in the shelter of the trees.

She was relieved to see that there was much less snow in the dense wood. She sat on a fallen log, took a breath, and tried not to think about what the last leg of the trip would be like once she had found the man she'd been sent for. It might be morning on the fields, but the pale winter light had not penetrated the forest. She suddenly felt terribly tired.

She took out her map and torch and opened the map to ascertain she was on the right track. With a little exclamation of victory, she smiled for the first time in some hours. Not only was she on the right track, but this was also the very elongated wood that passed all three of the little coves, including the one she was making for.

Sitting in the cold had made her limbs stiff. She got up and waved her arms about and lifted her feet, marching in place to get the blood flowing. Time to go see about those coves. She moved first in the direction of the water to see if she could figure out exactly where she was, and then she continued south along the edge of the trees. After what seemed a long distance, she stepped into the open and heard the water lapping at the shore below. She must be very close! The big worry now was how far her cove was from where she was standing.

The snow on this side of the wood was not as deep as it had been on the other side facing the exposed path on the open field. She moved cautiously toward the water and was relieved: the sound of lapping told her it was not far below her. Would it be safe to scramble down and walk along the shore itself? The tidal chart on the wall of the last inn had told her it would be low at 2300 hours. It would be steadily climbing after that, but with any luck still low enough to pull off the landing. But of course the Germans will have known the tides, planned for them. She looked at her watch and groaned. Not even seven in the morning. There was no point clattering about. She cursed the innkeeper for driving her out into the elements at three in the morning, leaving her with a whole day's worth of freezing hours to sit and wait in a forest, starving and without the benefit of even a cup of tea. She ducked back into the wood, found a downed tree in the tangle of forest, and dropped the backpack and irksome snowshoes.

There were a few evergreen branches perhaps blown off in a winter storm, and she piled them together as a seat. The protection of the dense stand of trees would keep the worst of the wind and weather at bay, should it begin to snow in earnest again. She dropped down with a sigh, leaning against the tree to think about what she would eat if she ever saw food again. Then she remembered the chocolates. There should be at least three left! She pulled open the ties of the rucksack and scrabbled around until she found the paper bag. There they were. Breakfast, lunch, and dinner? Or just one giant breakfast to make up for how annoyed she was? She needn't decide just yet. She would eat one very, very slowly and see how she got on.

If she had thought it delicious on the train with Freda, it was ten times more welcome and delectable now! She closed her eyes and imagined herself far away.

CHAPTER FOURTEEN

LANE WOKE WITH A START. It was dark. She'd spent the day moving to keep warm, going to the edge of the wood to look out at the fields and cottages, each with maddeningly enticing curls of smoke coming from their chimneys. She'd tried practicing all the Wordsworth and Gray she'd been made to memorize in school. Looking out on the fields again, misty still on this winter's day, she had certainly felt as lonely as a cloud. She had turned her mind then to Shakespeare, and worked her way through the story lines of his plays, even taking a stab at some soliloquies with some creative additions of her own. Finally, after a long day of many such exercises, her interrupted sleep had caught up with her and she had sat down to close her eyes for just a moment.

Experiencing a moment of panic, she looked at her watch, couldn't see it, reached for her torch, and then breathed a sigh of relief. It was a little after nine. Then in the next moment she was disappointed. Still four hours till the rendezvous. She stood and shook herself, feeling her limbs again stiff and icy with the cold. The tide would be out now, so she could find exactly where she had to be.

Deciding she'd better take her things in case she couldn't come back, she picked up her snowshoes, strapped them onto the backpack, and left the shelter of the forest, making toward the cliff down to the water.

With utmost caution she pushed her boot several times through the snow to make sure there was solid ground underneath, and carefully stepped forward until she could feel the edge. Now, even in the dark, she fancied she could see the snow end and the dark water begin some ten feet below. It was a steep drop. She thought she saw a ledge partway down. She sat down and began to descend carefully on her bottom until she reached the narrow rocky ledge. Seven feet more, maybe? She turned her body around until she lay on her stomach, her legs dangling over the ledge. She moved backward and down until her feet were touching the face of the drop to the beach below, and she cautiously felt about to find a foothold.

Just when she thought she'd found one, sudden emptiness met her foot. She slid down, unable to keep her grip with her gloves, banging her cheek on a rock on the way down. She landed on her back on the hard sand, her rucksack and snowshoes breaking the fall painfully. She took a long moment to catch her breath and then sat up and put her hand to her cheek. It hurt like the dickens, and she swore.

Scrambling to her feet, she scooped a handful of snow and placed it against her cheek, wincing at the sudden cold, but feeling it cool the burning of the abrasion. Well, she was here, and this was a little cove. But was it the right one?

With her ribs hurting where one of the snowshoes had jammed into her back, she walked toward the cliff edge that protruded to the south and found that, with the tide this low, it was possible to walk around it and into the next cove. Even in the dark, this cove appeared to be bigger than the one she'd landed in. She thought of the map. There had been a long sweeping cove, then a very deep narrow one, and then the one just south of that, where she was to meet the man. She longed to take out her map and torch, but if there were German submarines out there in the dark somewhere, she did not want to alert any that she was there.

Another quick exploration, and she exhaled a victorious breath of relief. Almost certainly the X-marks-the-spot cove was the next one over to the south. Nothing to do now but slip back there, find a cozy corner out of the worst of the weather, and wait, trying to work out how on earth they were to get back to her grandparents' cottage. It was at that moment she felt the first drop of rain.

HUDDLED INTO THE lee of the cliff, Lane damned all weather. She looked at her watch and frowned. Still almost an hour to go. An hour until Christmas Eve day. Time ground to a stop. She tried to focus on how they'd get away, but she couldn't organize any thought past the wet and cold. She closed her eyes and put her head on her knees. Why couldn't they have left her at her desk translating? She wasn't cut out for this. Her father was right.

No, what she wasn't cut out for was sitting in the icy rain in a remote part of Scotland in the middle of the night. Nobody was. She thought about what her father must do, day in and day out. He must have had to spend many, many hours in unpleasant places waiting for things. And if he were ever captured . . . she shuddered. Just one more reason not to become a spy, not that women would ever be allowed to. She closed her eyes and her mind drifted to Irene . . . why was Irene behaving so strangely, keeping things from her, sneaking into her things?

Her eyes flew open, and she stared into the darkness. What had she seen? There it was again. A light from the water, two or three hundred yards out. A signal! Was it Morse code? It was the only thing her father had taught her as a game when she was a child. She fished out her torch. She would wait for the next transmission. She didn't have to wait long. One flash only, so not Morse code. Then what?

She moved toward the gravelly edge of the water, wondering if she was meant to respond, when she stopped aghast, her heart thumping. Someone was right on this beach, large as life, responding to the submarine signal! Who? She pulled back against the cliff, barely daring to breathe. As if the rain weren't bloody well enough! Now this!

Barkley and whomever he'd got his information from had got it all wrong! There was someone else here to meet the man. What should she do? She froze with indecision. Think! Think! She watched the darkness where the signal had come from and waited. There it was again. A third time. She guessed there wouldn't be a fourth. Was this friend or foe? Had they sent him in case she botched the meeting? Or was this someone who knew her man was a double X and had been sent to intercept him?

She thought about Barkley, reluctant to send her, warning her not to make a complete cock-up of the thing. She peered through the dark veil of rain. Man or woman? Trousers, jacket, hat pulled low. Barkley *could* have sent someone else. He could have sent Irene, just to make sure. Was that why Irene had been listening at the door? Going through her things? She felt a wave of fury. She'd spent three days marching around in the snow and cold, enduring lecherous innkeepers just to cover in case Irene failed? She shook her head, recovering, watching the outline of the figure on the beach. No. Barkley hadn't known about this. This could be Irene acting on her own. She'd listened, had known that this man was to be recovered by the British, and had pipped them all! Or maybe Irene was a traitor?

Well, Lane had a job to do, and she was bloody well going to do it. She carefully took off her rucksack, found her pistol, and pocketed her torch. She took a deep breath and began to run softly along against the foot of the cliff, now thanking God for the rain covering the sound of her movements. If this was Irene, she'd know that Lane had been sent. If she was a traitor, she'd be armed and ready. When Lane thought she was more or less behind the person sending the signals, she waited, water running down her face, blurring her vision. The person was waiting too. Then at last, another sound.

Paddling, barely audible in the downpour. In the dark, she could see the outline of the figure on the beach moving forward, closer to the water's edge. More movement, bending, the sound of scraping, a second figure. Splashing as someone walked the last few feet in the water.

"Good. You are here."

Lane gasped and put her hand to her mouth to cover it. A woman all right! Speaking German! She knew that voice, she was sure of it, but in the utter confusion of the moment she couldn't place it. It must be Irene! No, that was mad. But Irene *did* speak German. Why else would she recognize the voice? She took a deep breath, hardly able to believe that her fantasy that Irene was a traitor might be true. Now what?

She leaned closer, waiting. Why had the man not responded? Finally, after an interminable silence, the man spoke, in German.

"Who are you?" He sounded utterly disconcerted. So, this was not what he had expected.

"I am your reception committee. We must go quickly." There was no response again.

"Come on. I have a house of safety." The woman again, impatient now. Then Lane felt a real thrill of horror. Not Irene, Freda? It was bloody Freda! Dressed in thick woollen trousers and a man's jacket. Freda working for the other side!

Lane didn't hesitate now. She moved quickly toward the figures, her gun at the ready, and stopped four feet away. Freda still had not turned to look. Perhaps in the rain she still hadn't heard. But the man had. She could just see his face. He had not been expecting Freda. He had been expecting her.

"I think I've hurt my bloody ankle," she said loudly and clearly. Freda whirled around, a gasp escaping her lips.

"Hello, Freda. I didn't expect to see you so soon. How did you get here, anyway? I found the trip quite challenging. No. Don't move. I have a gun." Lane lifted it, pointing it so Freda could see it. She looked at the man, the bobbing dinghy nearly obscured by darkness. "Gosh, coming ashore just like *Beowulf*, really, isn't it?" She brandished her gun again. "Step back."

The man suddenly spoke. He had a thick accent. "Let me have a look." And then as Freda swung back toward him, he tackled her. "Rope! In the boat!" he shouted in German over Freda's outraged cries of protest. Lane put her pistol in her pocket and rushed forward into the water to pull the dinghy onto the beach. With her torch, she found the coiled rope and handed it to the man, who now had Freda face down with her arms behind her back. He felt in her pockets, found another pistol, and threw it toward Lane.

Suddenly, a flashing signal from out in the water. The man turned. "Can you signal back?"

Lane turned on the torch once and waited. There was one wink from out at sea and then darkness. She prayed that they would think they had successfully dropped off their man and go away.

The man and Lane peered into the wet darkness, but there was no more from the submarine.

"What is your name?"

"Marc Nowak."

Lane nodded. It was the name Barkley had given.

"Well, what now? Do you too have a 'house of safety' for me?" Nowak asked in German. He sounded angry. This reception was nothing like what he'd expected.

"Untie me at once!" Freda spluttered from where she still lay face down in the sand. "I work for the British government!"

Lane ignored her. She was thinking. Finally, she spoke. "We'd better take the dinghy and go north to the harbour at Eyemouth. The streets may be better now with the rain. We'll have to take her with us. I passed the police station on my way here. We'll say we found her trying to signal a German sub from our caravan, where I took you to recover. Once we've handed her to the police, let's hope the streets are passable, so we can find a bus or some other means of transport."

It was a business getting Freda into the dinghy. She kicked and fought.

"Please, Freda. It's over. I don't want to leave you here in the elements tied up like this." With ill grace, Freda consented to getting into the dinghy and sat scowling, water dripping down her face because she'd lost her hat. Lane had run back to the foot of the cliff to collect her rucksack, abandoning the snowshoes. No matter what the conditions, she was not going to resort to them again.

Marc Nowak pushed the dinghy with the two women in it farther into the water and then hopped in himself, causing it to rock wildly. The rain did not let up.

"Why, Freda?" Lane asked sadly as Nowak rowed through the dark. "You have everything. A wealthy, privileged family, education, a future."

"A future in this country? Don't make me laugh. Look around you. It is filled with degeneracy. We need to bring back order. And I told you already. There's no hope of winning this war. Germany will win, and I will be on the right side of history. And you!" She thrashed in desperation at her confinement and spat in the man's direction. "You are a traitor!"

The man did not respond.

"Pot calling the kettle black, I'd have said," Lane said with a sigh. "I honestly didn't know you spoke German. Did you already know at university that you would do this?"

Freda shrugged. "The writing was on the wall even then."

"Your parents must be very proud." Lane did not succeed in keeping the acid out of her tone.

"My parents do not understand anything. They will be swept away along with all that is wrong with this country."

Lane nodded. Freda seemed to have gone right over, as her grandmother used to say when she thought someone was barmy. "I suppose you lied about the ambulance driving as well. It's too bad. I really admired you for that."

Freda clamped her mouth shut and stared out to sea, ignoring the pelting rain.

The downpour did not let up. They travelled in silence but for the sound of the rain and Marc's efforts at rowing. Finally, Lane said, "Here. We can row into the harbour along here."

The entrance to the harbour was completely dark, and though the harbour buildings loomed out of the blackness, there was no light in any of them. Expecting, Lane thought, an invasion from the air, little knowing there was likely a slow drip of invasion seeping right in through their own protected coves.

CHAPTER FIFTEEN

"**M**Y HUSBAND AND I WERE in a caravan. I'm sorry, he can't speak and has trouble sleeping because of his shell shock. He's a navigator, and their bomber crashed," Lane extemporized hurriedly.

There was no point in saying Marc was her fiancé. There could be no question of an unmarried couple in a caravan together. "The quiet was recommended by his doctor." She shook her head. "I must say, I don't recommend caravanning in the worst snow in years. Anyway, he couldn't sleep in the middle of the night, and we were looking out to sea, and we saw the signals from out in the water, and then, much to our surprise, an answer from the beach below us. He said we had to get down and see who was signalling them from our shore. We found her." Lane pointed at Freda. "We sort of tackled her and took her torch so she couldn't send any more messages and tied her up and brought her here."

The constable they had woken from a deep sleep at the little Eyemouth station house frowned at them all. This could be the invasion. He'd have to be alert.

"You could all be German for all I know."

"I am not German, and I demand to be released," Freda

interjected. "I work for the British government. You have no right to hold me!"

"As you can see, Constable, my husband is in the Air Force. I beg you to trust me. This woman was signalling to someone out at sea."

The constable rubbed his chin with his hand. "I reckon there's no reason to untie you just at this moment," he said to Freda. "I've a couple of cells here. You can sleep it off in here, and we can sort it in the morning. You lot can go in the other cell."

Damn! Lane thought. She didn't blame him. The whole thing must seem completely suspicious to him. "Are you on the telephone, Constable? I must phone my grandmother in Broughton. I think I'd best take poor Marc there. I'm afraid he'll catch a chill, and in his condition, it could be fatal."

"Broughton? You know the place? My aunt has a bakery there, though fat lot she gets to bake now with the rationing."

"Would that be Mrs. Elkin, at the Grange?" Golly, she hoped it was.

"You know her?" The constable seemed relieved. "Opened the place years ago when she married Elkin. They both come from here. Well, he's dead now, but she's ticking over nicely."

"Of course I know her. I moved my grandparents there just a little over a year ago, and we had lovely things from the Grange!" She could use some lovely things from the bakery right this minute, she thought. She couldn't remember when she'd last had anything besides orange-filled chocolates.

"Go on, love. Telephone is just over there." The constable pointed at the wall, his voice sympathetic now. The fact of

Lane knowing his aunt seemed all the reassurance he needed, and Lane, praying that someone would answer the telephone at 4:30 in the morning, put in her call to Broughton.

"As for you, young lady, let's get you settled in here." The constable led Freda, the protest apparently gone out of her, to the tiny cell and locked her in. "Turn around. I'll untie you. I've got a couple of blankets for you. We'll see what's what in the morning. Sir, you have a seat over there by the stove," he added kindly to Marc, who really was looking the worse for wear.

Lane had got through. "Grandmama, it's Lane. I'm terribly sorry to wake you at this ungodly hour. I'm just up in Eyemouth with Marc. He's not feeling very well. He's got a terrible chill." Lane hoped that behind her Marc was playing the part of a man with a terrible chill. "I'm hoping to find a bus or something to get him down there first thing when it's light."

She listened. The people in the room with her could hear the tinny sound of a voice on the other end. "You were up? Yes, Grandmama, we'll do our best. Yes. The doctor will be a good idea. I'll explain everything when I get there."

Lane rang off, comforted by the sound of her grandmother's voice, and she turned back to where Marc was sitting, slumped now in the chair near the fire, his eyes closed. She wondered suddenly why her grandmother would be up at 4:30 in the morning, but she pushed this thought aside.

The constable nodded at her. "My cousin is driving up to his parents' farm past Broughton there. I don't know how good the roads are. That deep snow we have with the rain is a rare bad mix, but his lorry has seen worse."

Lane's heart leaped. "Oh, do you think he'd be willing to take us? I'd be happy to give him something for the trouble."

"I'm sure he'd appreciate that. He won't be up for another hour or so. You make yourselves comfortable and I'll put the kettle on."

Lane sat down next to Marc, elated at the idea of tea, but feeling the stuffing come out of her all at once. She was exhausted, starving, wet, and cold. Out of the rain though they may be, the warmth was paltry because the fire in the stove had been banked for the night. The cottage felt like an icebox. She glanced enviously at their prisoner, who had the benefit of the blankets she'd been given. Freda sat rigid with anger, blankets wrapped tightly around her, staring straight ahead.

Lane thought about Freda. She had heard of other people who were pro-German. Before the war, businesspeople and people in the upper echelons of society had wined and dined their Nazi visitors. There'd been a fascist movement in the country since the 1920s. But with Freda it hadn't been her family, if what she said was to be believed. She had developed this passion—Lane wondered briefly for what . . . order, she supposed?—all on her own. Or perhaps it was the despair Freda had expressed on their train ride together that they had no hope of winning against Germany. If you can't beat them, join them, sort of thing.

She was surprised to see Freda suddenly lean forward and look straight at Marc. "You are a traitor," she hissed in a loud whisper in German. "They will find you and execute you! I should have shot you at once!" She turned away in disgust.

"Well, well," said the constable, who was just coming in with some mugs. "You know, I was in there, wondering what to believe about all this. We've got to be very careful nowadays, what with the constant threat of invasion. Maybe this young lady is right, I told myself. Maybe she does work for the British government, and you two are the enemy, except that you know my aunt. But I think I've heard enough, her talking German like that. I don't speak it myself, so I can't say what she said. But I know the German lingo when I hear it."

Lane was itching to utter a sarcastic, "Oh, well done, Freda," but refrained. Really, Freda had caused quite a lot of extra trouble, all in all.

"Don't worry, love, I'll still give you a cup of tea," he said to Freda as he disappeared into the kitchen again. "We aren't barbarians here," he called from the next room. He came back out with a large brown teapot covered in a nicely crocheted tea cozy. "Just good old Brits trying to keep our country safe. No sugar, I'm afraid. I tried in the shops yesterday, but it was gone. I have honey, though. My cousin, that same one with the lorry, he's got some bees."

With a cheerfulness that belied the situation, the constable—called Hickling, they discovered—poured tea and mixed quite substantial spoons of honey into each mug.

Really, Lane thought watching this simple, practical, kind man, we are a little like hobbits. She'd read Tolkien's children's book at Oxford and had found it charming. Of course, we are innocent no more. She sighed and thought about the incessant bombing of London and Liverpool and the other industrial cities. How would it ever be made to stop? Could a man like this, with his tea and honey, really be any defense in the end against the overwhelming ferocity of their enemy?

She drew herself up short. Now she was in danger of falling into despair, as Freda had. One thing she knew, though, was that she would never fall as far as her erstwhile friend.

SIX IN THE morning, Christmas Eve, Lane thought, amazed at how significant this day had been in her childhood, and how dismal it appeared now. Then, it had sparked a feeling of almost overwhelming anticipation. The whole day in her grandmother's house suffused with candles and oranges, laughter and cake, and playing outside with her little sister and Ganf, and even some of his maiden sisters, her timorous great-aunts, exhilarated by the snow and the sheer magic of the day.

Now, the small window showed an unrelenting grey sky and a wet, slushy street with no one abroad but the constable's lorry-driving cousin, his arms wrapped around him, coming up the path trying to avoid the deeper puddles of icy water. God bless Constable Hickling's family, and long may they live! Lane thought.

"Aye," he said. "I can squeeze you two in the cabin. It'll be a tight fit, but we'll see how we go. I promised my auntie I'd try to get to her today."

"Will you be going via Edinburgh?" Lane asked.

"The only way, what with the roads. More traffic."

"Would it be possible to stop at the White Hart just outside the city? I've left something there. It would be the work of a moment to run in and get it."

"Oh, aye. I don't see why not."

Lane turned to Freda. She was lying now, the blankets pulled around her, sound asleep, her beautiful gold hair out of its bun and falling around her face. "Goodbye, Freda," she whispered sadly.

GANF AND MRS. Andrews were sitting in front of the fire wrapped in thick woollen robes, with their slippered feet toward the flames. The clattering of crockery sounded from the kitchen down the passage, and a muffled cry of "Ouch!"

"It's a cruelty to make her get up this early. I was quite prepared to do it myself," Mrs. Andrews said. "Poor Alice has become most devoted. I don't know what we'll do when her young man comes to claim her."

Ganf shook his head. "If he comes, poor chap. But we are not saying poor Alice anymore, are we? Magnificent Alice, more like it. And anyway, I soon expect to see her sawdust and gun oil biscuits in the newspaper in the women's section: 'Scottish housewives make do in wartime: Use common household ingredients for these delicious biscuits.'"

The sound of Alice with the tea made its way up the passage. "Do we think she'll really be here early?" she asked. "It's dreadful out there. I wouldn't go out in that if you paid me."

"And no one will make you, Alice," said Ganf kindly. "Oh, splendid! A cup of tea can fight off all evils." They'd bundled their guest onto the settee, but he appeared to still be asleep.

When a third chair had been pulled up to the fire and

they all had a cup, Ganf raised his and said, "Happy Christmas Eve!"

The sound of a motor grinding up the hill and stopping made them all look up. Ganf went to the window. "It's one of those American Jeeps," he said. "They'd be champion in territory like this. I expect it's your chum, Major Flint." He moved to the settee and shook the prisoner. "Wake up. Your transport has come." He opened the front door and waved as the major and an enlisted man came up the walk. "Come in, come in! You made it."

"Thank you, Mr. Andrews. The snow is going to ease up a bit. It's warming up and there's rain forecast. It'll be beastly, slushy going, but the roads might be passable again for regular vehicles. Now then, your guest." Major Flint removed his cap and wiped his feet on the rug by the door and his enlisted man followed suit. Once inside, the private stood respectfully behind his commander, turning his hat in his hand and looking with interest at the blanketed man scowling at them from the settee, where he was now sitting up.

"He's got a bang on the head, I'm afraid, Major Flint, so probably a headache as well as the gash on his leg."

"We'll give him some Aspirin," said Flint, looking at the prisoner without warmth.

"Will you take a cup of tea?" Mrs. Andrews asked.

"Nothing we'd like better, but I think we'd better get this chap out of your hair and back to the police in Edinburgh. It's going to be a good three hours or more in this. It took us that long to get here." He looked at the Andrewses and gave his head a little shake. "I must say, you've done a splendid job. Herr Hitler will have a hard time getting past you two!"

The prisoner looked away with an exasperated expression and gave a little shake of the head.

"Oh, not really us at all. It was Alice." She walked to the passage and called, "Alice, can you come here a minute?"

Alice hurried out from where she'd been listening behind the kitchen door, pretending to wipe her hands on her apron. She eyed the men's wet boots with disapproval.

"Alice, this is Major Flint, and . . . ?"

"Private Jenkins, ma'am," said the young man.

"And Private Jenkins," Mrs. Andrews continued. "This is Alice, who had the presence of mind to whack . . . I'm sorry, he's not given us his name . . . on the head, which incapacitated him enough for my husband to tie him up. Oh, and by the way, he speaks perfect English. He's a Cambridge man, he tells us."

"Ah," Flint said, looking with interest at the prisoner. "What made you think he wasn't English?"

"This," said Ganf, moving to the desk and pulling out the Luger. "He poked me in the chest with it when I went out to the shed to get firewood. He had a bit of bad luck coming down. The trouser leg of his almost British uniform was badly torn. His pips are all wrong, if you look at the insignia on his tunic. Entirely bogus. Don't know how they thought they'd get anyone through, wearing those things. He demanded his bag and generally made a nuisance of himself."

Flint peered closely at the prisoner's collar. "You're absolutely right. Well spotted! It's that sort of carelessness that's been letting them down from the start." He turned to the scowling man. "Ah, you knew these people had your bag then, did you?"

"My name is Rudy Weiss. I am an ss Hauptscharfürer, serial number 83295. I demand consideration as a prisoner of war."

"My dear chap, you're in no position to demand anything. Come on, up you get." Flint removed the blanket, took one arm, and nodded at Jenkins to get the other, and they lifted the man to his feet. Jenkins handed Alice the blanket with a little wink, causing her to blush violently. Flint looked at the tying-up job Ganf had done and nodded in approval. "Quite professional. Now, I believe you have this man's bag. We'd better take that along as well. He'd have had a difficult time without it. It would have contained maps, compasses, concealed weapons."

"Oh," Ganf said, surprised. "I just found English matches and cigarettes and hairbrushes and so on. Toiletries. And, I must say, a funny toothbrush."

"Exactly," said Flint, smiling and tapping the side of his nose. "Ah, splendid." He took the bag from Mrs. Andrews. "Thank you very much. You've saved us a lot of grief. If he'd escaped, he could have done untold damage. Get him out there," he said to his subordinate. "Would you mind if I used your telephone to call the authorities in Edinburgh? They've had reports of this character as well. I can let them know to stand down."

"Please," said Ganf, showing him the instrument.

The three of them stood at the window watching Flint and Jenkins lead Rudy Weiss away, bag and Luger in tow.

"I suppose it's terribly brave to go on your own into enemy territory," Mrs. Andrews said. "I don't think I'd do it."

"I don't think he's all that bright," Ganf declared. "He speaks perfect English. He could have taken a stab at pretending to be a wounded airman. But I tell you who is brave. Our Alice! How did you know to sneak along the passage with a filthy great frying pan?"

"I was in the pantry and saw you through the kitchen window, sir, with that man and his gun. When I saw you come into the sitting room, I got my pan and signalled to Mrs. Andrews, and she kept him talking."

"I think we should celebrate," Ganf said, looking with admiration at his wife and rubbing his hands together. "What about a bit of that cake?"

IT WAS ALMOST noon, though in fairness it was barely discernible in the unremitting grey from outside, when Mrs. Andrews, encased in a thick tweed skirt, wool stockings, and several layers of jumpers, looked up from her knitting.

"I hear a lorry!" she cried excitedly. Dropping the knitting into its basket, she rushed to the window. Ganf had been in the room they used as a library and came out to join her. Alice, who had prepared the rooms for the visitors, stood beside them.

The lorry, a green affair with a wood slat bed, struggled up the hill and stopped in front of the gate. The passenger door opened and a man in a blue Air Force uniform got out, followed by Lane, who turned back to say something to the driver. The man went around the back of the truck and pulled off a suitcase. As they watched, Lane reached into her rucksack, pulled out money, and handed it in to the driver.

Ganf threw open the door and cried, "Welcome! Welcome, my darling girl!"

Lane hurried up the stairs and threw herself into his arms. "Happy Christmas, dearest Ganf! Oh, and darling Grandmama . . ." But she could say no more as she was smothered in a woolly embrace.

When they were in the little foyer, Alice stood with her hands on her waist looking at their boots.

"Hello, Alice," Lane said with a warm smile. "Yes, yes, boots off! Such a dragon about boots! It's so lovely to see you. Are my grandparents treating you well?"

"Oh, wonderfully, miss, thank you."

Boots off, they all now stood in the sitting room. "Now then," Lane said. "This is Marc Nowak. He is from my office in London and helps with the work we do. He speaks a little English and a little German and a lot of Polish, so we should get along splendidly. We got a ride from the train station in Edinburgh, but it was beastly, and we had to get out and push once. That's why we're still rather damp."

"Ah," said Ganf. "No wonder you look like wet cats. Alice, will you show Mr. Nowak up to his room? I'll be right up with some warm dry clothes for you to wear. We're about the same size."

"Thank you," Marc said in accented English. He followed the slightly nervous Alice up the stairs. He was foreign and she didn't hold with foreigners, except that this one was very handsome.

"Look at all this!" Lane cried in delight, waving at the

boughs along the mantel and shelves, and the lovely old Christmas cards. In the corner stood a very small tree in a wooden stand still unadorned. "Ooh! I have just the thing for that! I wasn't sure if you had candles for the brass holders, and I found some at Fortnum's."

"Is he all right, your friend?" Mrs. Andrews asked.

Lane turned to look at her grandmother. Always kind. Another safe harbour in this sea of troubles. "I think so, Grandmama. He is rather like one of Daddy's friends, if you know what I mean." She could say no more than that, and indeed worried that she'd said too much.

Her grandmother glanced toward the stairs and nodded. They could hear the low murmur of voices and the sound of footsteps above them.

Marc had collapsed on the bed and sat exhaustedly with his elbows on his knees, looking down at the floor.

"You have had a difficult journey," Ganf said in German. He was holding a folded pile of clothing, which he laid on the bed next to their guest.

Marc looked up in surprise and then nodded. He appeared nervous, perhaps disoriented. "We have not slept since . . . I arrived."

"Please don't worry, Marc. We all speak German here. We have only recently come from our British community in Latvia. Except Alice, the girl who helps us, and she is very suspicious, as you can imagine. Now then. Make yourself comfortable. You will find a bathroom and a toilet down the hall. Here are your towels. No electrics, though, so we can't manage a bath just at the moment."

"Thank you," Marc said in English. "Thank you." He nodded, exhaustion overwhelming him. "You are . . . thank you."

CHAPTER SIXTEEN

"**HAVE YOU HEARD FROM HER?**"

Smithers turned down his mouth and looked around Barkley's office. He didn't like disorder, and Barkley was disorderly. "No, sir. Not yet. The pickup was meant to be at 0100 last night. The weather has been beastly. I don't know if she even got there." He sighed and rattled the change in his pockets. "I wasn't in favour of sending an untried girl on this job, but I do see it would arouse less suspicion, and she speaks German."

"Well, no need to panic yet. But if it didn't come off, we'll have the poor chap wandering around the countryside on his own. I don't give him an hour with the level of suspicion among the populace. I suppose if he doesn't get shot by some overzealous citizen, he might be arrested, and we'll get our hands on him eventually anyway."

"It was mighty busy in that quadrant. We did arrest someone. One of our own, signalling to an enemy submarine. Girl from a toff family, if you can believe it. They're the worst! Do you know the Beauvilles? Been here since the conquest."

"I don't, no, but I can imagine. Like the bloody

Mosleys! But you say she was signalling from a beach. Who found her?"

"Don't know the whole story. Wounded airman and his wife strolling on the beach, brought her in. Caught her red-handed."

"Lucky for us they were on hand." But in the back of Barkley's mind, all unbidden, came the thought, I wonder . . . ?

"Funnily enough a couple of old people managed to get hold of a German spy who was hiding in their woodshed. Hit him on the head, tied him up, and delivered him to the local authorities. Same area. Up in—" Smithers consulted the topmost of a thin sheaf of papers. "Broughton. Border country. That's what I mean. If our man isn't picked up by your girl, he doesn't stand a snowball's chance in hell with those people. God bless 'em!"

FREDA HELD THE receiver in her hand. "Uncle, yes. I'm sorry to bother you in the morning like this. I've had a spot of trouble, and the police here seem to have got the wrong end of the stick. They seem to think I'm some sort of enemy alien. Could you have a word?"

She handed the receiver to Chief Constable Rutgers of the Edinburgh police. "It's my uncle, the Honourable F. Francis, KC."

She stood listening to her end of the conversation, Rutgers glancing at her once or twice. "We understood she was found by some citizens apparently signalling a German submarine, sir. They brought her in at the Eyemouth constabulary who sent her to us here first thing." He nodded and listened. His expression became anxious. "There'll be no need for that, sir. Yes, sir. I'm sure there is a ready explanation." Then he looked up at the clock. "There should be no difficulty getting her to you on time for lunch, sir." He nearly chuckled at this point, as if Christmas Eve lunch were the greatest joke in the world.

"Well, young lady. You're free to go. Your uncle vouches for you. It's the times, I suppose. Everyone is a bit jumpy. I'm sure you don't blame those citizens for thinking they were doing the right thing. It's a waste of time, if you want the truth. This weather has caused chaos everywhere, and we need to be ready for real spies. They just got one out in Broughton, if you can believe it. A couple of old people called Andrews. He turned out to be the genuine item. They're just now going to try to get through the snow to get him here." He shook his head. "Oh, I didn't ask the gentleman where we should put you down. We have a Land Rover that will do the job."

Freda, scarcely able to believe her luck, said, with all the charm she could muster, "Are you sure? Funnily, it is right near Broughton. There's a manor house a mile off the road. That's where my lunch is, and I must say, I'm beginning to look forward to it!"

Outside, she turned and shook the hand of the chief constable. "Thank you so very much. I am sorry to have been such a nuisance. I really thought I was for it this morning! And I must say, in this climate I wouldn't have blamed you one bit. With the alertness of the citizenry, we're bound to keep the blighters out of the country!"

The CC helped her into the vehicle and was about to

shut the door when he said, "What were you doing out there, anyway?"

She tried to still her anxiety as the Rover roared and bumped along the snowy road, but near the crest of a hill, she finally saw what she was looking for. "Just here, thank you, constable. It's just a short way up that lane, and as you can see, it's been driven on, so I'll have no trouble walking it."

She watched the Land Rover turn awkwardly between the banks of snow and begin its journey back and was soon on her own. It was a gamble. Well, the whole thing had been. She was amazed the chief constable had swallowed her story about losing a valuable piece of jewellery on the beach earlier that evening, and being terrified that with the rising tide, it would be lost forever.

She looked down the road in the direction of Broughton. They'd passed no other traffic, so with any luck, she was not too late. She struggled through the snow the few yards to the very crest of the hill, which lay adjacent to a small stand of trees, and sat down to watch the road below her, smiling. They hadn't found her tidy little Beretta 418 in its makeshift holster strapped under her shirt.

"WE HAD SUCH an adventure you will never guess!" said Mrs. Andrews. Lane and her grandparents were sitting before the fire. Lane had run up to her room to unpack and change into dry warm clothes and had brought down the candles. Their guest had been heard washing his face and then disappearing into his room for a nap.

"Poor man," Ganf said. "We've no electricity, so that

lovely new electric boiler you got for us is useless. I'll get Alice to boil up a couple of pots so he can have a bit of warm water to wash up with tonight."

Her grandparents got back to the job at hand, recounting their thrilling story of the lost "airman," only to find he was a German spy, and how he'd been collected by Major Flint from the local air base.

"Gosh, that is an adventure! Thank heaven for Alice!" Lane exclaimed. "I knew she had good stuff in her the minute I laid eyes on her." She settled more deeply into the chair and stared at the fire, thinking of her own adventure—one she would not be able to talk about at all, and in truth, one she could still scarcely comprehend. The thought that her friend Freda actually had turned her back on her country! She shook her head and snuggled into the chair. The fire burbled cheerfully, blissfully warm after her long ordeal and giving her a momentary feeling of being safe.

"I wonder what's happened to our spy. He was called Rudy. I wonder if I ought to telephone the base and talk with Major Flint," Mrs. Andrews said into the quiet.

"I'm sure they won't tell you a thing," Ganf said. "Much more important is how Alice is going to assemble our Christmas lunch." He turned to Lane. "Your Grandmama taught her to make a Christmas cake. Whether the instruction goes in one ear and out the other we will not know, but I feel some dawning hope that Alice may one day get the knack. I got a nice goose from a local farm, and they were kind enough to throw in some potatoes and carrots from their winter supplies. I wouldn't like to have it charred."

"Will Alice not be at home with her family for Christmas?"

Lane asked, hoping that she would not be enlisted to try to roast a goose. She had only ever been on the eating side of the equation.

"No. She asked if she could stay with us. I think she has to share a small room and cope with a lot of siblings, and she finds it much quieter here. Besides, she loves lording it over the kitchen, however inadequate her skills. Apparently, her mother has given her instructions for the goose roasting."

"Then I am happy I bought her a little present." Lane glanced at her grandmother, who still sat looking thoughtfully into the fire, as if she were somewhere else. "It can't hurt to give them a call. The worst you'll hear is 'no.'"

"I will at that. I don't know why it's niggling at me like this." Mrs. Andrews got up and crossed to the desk and began to put in the call.

"Your Grandmama and her niggles! Last time she had a niggle she began to pack. 'Something bad is going to happen,' she said. Next thing you know, we are told of an impending Russian occupation. Thanks to your father, who acted quickly to get us out of there, here we are."

"Gosh, I hope this isn't that serious a niggle!" Lane exclaimed. She turned to look at where her grandmother stood, holding the earpiece to her ear, and gripping the stem of the phone tightly in her other hand, waiting to be put through. It was early afternoon, but the light was already fading outside.

Ganf got up with an *oof* and said, "I'd better get the lamps going."

"Yes, good afternoon," Mrs. Andrews was saying into the horn. "I wonder if I might speak to Major Flint?" After some moments she turned to look at the gathering in the sitting room, her brow knitted in alarm. "But that can't be. He was here only this morning." Pause. She collapsed into the desk chair. "But what does this mean?" Pause. She glanced toward the door. "Of course. Yes, we will, of course." She put the phone down, hung the receiver on the hook, and rang off.

"Major Flint is in sick bay, beaten to within an inch of his life, and left for dead," she said. "They found the Jeep, Flint badly beaten, poor Jenkins shot and clinging to life, and the prisoner gone!"

"That beastly man got free and overcame both of them?" Ganf asked, horrified.

His wife nodded numbly. "It would seem so, though I can't think how."

Ganf looked despairing. "This was my fault! I didn't tie him up properly!"

"I'm sure it's not your fault. Someone must have been waiting for them, freed him."

"The doors!" Ganf exclaimed. "Lock them at once! If I'm not wrong, we shall need to look after your party." He gave Lane a significant look.

Lane looked at her watch. Nearly five. "Look, I must use the telephone, and I'm afraid I shall need privacy. Even my humble job is under the hat, I'm afraid."

"Yes, of course," her grandmother said. "Come on, you lot. Off to the kitchen. We can check the doors and begin to think about Christmas lunch tomorrow."

She was the last to leave, and Lane stopped her, whispering, "What was that German's surname?"

"Oh, let me think. Rudy, Rudy . . . Weiss. That was it."

Lane nodded and made for the desk. After ten agonizing minutes she was connected to Barking—no, she must stop doing that. Barkley, she corrected inwardly. "It's Lane Winslow," she said.

"'Bout time," he barked. All right. Maybe she wouldn't stop. "What have you got to say?"

"I've got our man to Broughton. We are at my grandmother's, but there was a bump or two in the road. For one thing, there was a woman at the beach signalling the submarine in German. She had clearly been sent by someone to meet Marc as well. We managed to get her to the local authorities in Eyemouth, and though she was British, she convinced them she was on the wrong side by suddenly speaking German to Marc. That's how we got here with no trouble. However, there has been trouble here as well. A German managed to fall into the local wood with his parachute and fetched up in my grandparents' woodshed because my grandmother found his bag in the wood. He wanted it back and was prepared to do anything for it with his Luger. Their cook cracked him on the head when he wasn't looking, my grandfather tied him up, and my grandmother called the local air base and got a Major Flint to come get him. Well, she just called the base to see what happened—" In the pause, Lane sighed.

"None of their business what happened."

"I understand, sir, but we've just learned the man got loose and left his escort for dead. I don't know how he got out of their custody."

Another long silence. "I do," Barkley said tightly.

"Sir? You knew?" Lane asked. She sensed he might be reluctant to go on, but if the village was swimming with German agents who might put her grandparents in danger . . .

"That girl you caught. The police in Edinburgh let her go. They assumed the local bobby was being overzealous and she convinced them of her bona fides."

"That's the problem! There's nothing wrong with her bloody bona fides!" Lane exclaimed, outraged. "She's a posh girl from a posh family. But she's also a traitor! Are you saying she's the one who freed Rudy Weiss?"

"Flint came to an hour ago and told them what happened. That means there are two dangerous people abroad up there. I suspect she will take him to her estate west of Edinburgh. I've dispatched someone there. She won't suspect that we know where that is, and with any luck we catch them . . . oh . . . one moment, Winslow."

Lane could hear him clamp his hand over the mouthpiece of the phone in his office and then heard muffled voices. She waited, thinking of the beautiful and seemingly very accomplished Freda Beauville. Women ought to be conscripted as spies, she thought. A beautiful woman like her could talk her way out of anything. Imagine if we put women like that in Europe?

"Bloody hell," Barkley said, back.

"What?"

"They aren't there because our driver put her down, at her request, near Broughton. Damn! She bloody well knew where to intercept Flint!"

"Look, she was trying to pick up the same man I was.

That must mean they want him and are looking for him. They must know he's a double X. It won't be long before they find their way here."

"I was just going to say that, Winslow, if you'd let me speak." Barkley sounded irritated about being cut off by Lane. "The question is, do they know where you are now?"

Lane hesitated. "I'm afraid they might. Freda knows where my grandparents live."

"Brilliant. Absolutely bloody brilliant."

"I wonder, sir . . ."

"What do you wonder? I haven't got all night."

"If Freda and the real German spy are loose, would they be on a mission to eliminate Marc, or just capture him?"

"They'll want to get information from him, but either one is out of the question. He'll have to be secured immediately. If he's captured he'll reveal our entire . . . Never mind. Just guard him with your life!"

"I think we can keep him secure until you get someone here, sir. We have the weapon you kindly gave me, and my grandfather has one and is an excellent shot."

"Why does this Beauville woman know where your grandparents live?" he asked angrily.

"I know her, sir. I was at Oxford with her before I was called up. In fact, she was on the same train I was, coming to Edinburgh. She said she was visiting her family. I had no reason to doubt her. I was shocked to see her signalling a German submarine."

"Bloody women," Barkley exclaimed furiously. "I'm going to try to get someone to you as quickly as possible."

"Yes, sir. We've locked the doors and will let no one in.

When can you get someone here?"

"My God, this is a nightmare! I don't know. As fast as I can. Just try to hang on to this man. An absolute bloody nightmare!" With that, Barkley rang off.

Honestly, Lane thought, we're in the middle of the nightmare here, while he's sitting in London, cool as you please in a nice quiet office!

All right. That wasn't fair. London was being bombed to smithereens every night. She sighed and got up. She'd have to talk to Marc immediately. She ran up the stairs and rapped quietly on his door.

"*Ya?*"

"Marc, may I come in?" She said this in English, in case she was in earshot of Alice.

"*Ya, ya.* Come." He sounded sleepy.

Lane pushed the door open and found him sitting up on the bed wiping sleep from his eyes. He was dressed in her grandfather's clothes. Speaking quietly in German, she told him about the situation with Freda.

"His name is Rudy Weiss. Do you know him?" She wasn't sure if that was even his real name.

Marc's hand flew up to smack his forehead. "*Mój Boże!*" he exclaimed. "Of course I know him! He is in my unit. He is a die-hard Nazi. He will mean harm, and if he is with her, he might . . . no, he will . . . be looking for me. He must have suspected I am no longer loyal to the Reich. Now he will know this for sure. I must leave here at once or you and your family are in great danger!" He jumped up and began to throw his things into his bag.

"No. Sit down, Marc, please," Lane said, pulling gently

on the sleeve of the pullover he was wearing. "Now that we know the danger, you are safer here. We have several firearms, the doors are locked, and we will admit no one. You must wait until my people come for you. My superior said they will come as soon as they can." She smiled. "Anyway, it is Christmas Eve. We are going to put candles on the tree and have cake and sing a little."

When they came downstairs, her grandparents were again at the fireplace, a bottle of sherry and five little glasses on a tray.

"It is all right. We are going to wait and let no one in. Let's enjoy our Christmas Eve. Someone will come for Marc as soon as possible. Ganf, do you have a revolver? Can you still shoot?" He had belonged to a shooting club in Bulduri and was second place twice in the annual contest.

"Really, you can ask that? I'm a champion shot," he said. "I have my own pistol. Your father gave it to me before we came here. A little Webley 2 from the war. He didn't want us unprotected back home. I don't expect he thought we'd need it here! Now then. Alice has prepared some sort of dish with sticks and beans and roots for our supper, so we will prepare ourselves with a little sherry. One only hopes a little will be enough for whatever awaits us from that quarter! You look splendid in those clothes, Marc. I'm glad they fit."

The room was snug indeed, with the fire and the thick blackout curtains drawn across the windows, the soft yellow light of the lantern playing on the walls. Lane leaned back in her chair and lifted her glass. "To our side," she said.

CHAPTER SEVENTEEN

AFTER SUPPER WHEN ALICE HAD cleared away the dishes, Grandmama said, "Now, the tree. Our little *Weihnachtsbaum*. Lanette, dear, the brass holders are in the hall in a shoebox on the top shelf, and there should be a box of ornaments. Alice, will you bring the cake and some plates? Then we can all get to work here."

The tree was standing by the desk in front of the window with its blackout curtains. Alice fitted the candles into the brass holders, and Lane and Mrs. Andrews balanced them carefully on the tree. Ganf and Marc went through the box of ornaments and chose a few. It was not, after all, an enormous tree. When it was finished, they all stood back to admire it.

"Well, shall we?" Ganf said, pulling a box of safety matches out of his pocket.

For the first time, Lane began to feel that old anticipation she'd loved so much as a child. "Wait!" she said. "Shouldn't we put some presents under the tree? Grandmama . . . do you have anything to wrap with? Some brown paper and string?"

"And I have a few little presents, as well," her grandmother said. "Yes. All right. Gosh, the war makes you forget the niceties! You two gentlemen sit by the fire and keep it company. Ganf, don't you have some brandy?"

"So I do," he said. "Come along, Marc. Let's leave the ladies to it."

"It is almost like home," Marc said quietly in German when the women had scattered to their various rooms. "Or perhaps I mean like what used to be home. Our home is in enemy hands. But before, my mother used to make a beautiful Christmas Eve. We would go to mass at midnight . . ." He sighed and accepted a glass of brandy.

"May I ask? How did you become a German agent?" Ganf asked.

"What?" Marc asked in surprise. He looked toward the hallway. "She told you this?"

Ganf shook his head. "No, forgive me. She would certainly say nothing. This sort of work runs in the family, you might say. I suspected it from the start."

Marc shrugged. "I thought at first that I must join them if I and my family were to survive. I speak German and a little English. They saw us as perfect people to infiltrate because England already was having Polish refugees. So, I agreed. Or at least, I pretended to. I am worried that Rudy Weiss has found out. It means they know I am a double agent. If they are not caught, they will track me until they find out all I know and kill me. And even if they do not succeed in eliminating me, it will get back to Germany, then I will be of no use to the British." He drank back the brandy. "Maybe I will work on a farm somewhere like all the other countrymen who are here. At least I can contribute a little. If I survive."

They sat in silence for some moments. "The world is in a pickle," Ganf said. "Everything that was is turned over, destroyed, the whole world that used to be is gone forever, all because of the greed of one man." He lifted the bottle and poured more brandy. "It has convinced me like nothing else can that all we ever have is this moment. We spend too much time remembering the past and thinking the future will be same forever. We miss what is right now. And right now is . . . ah, the ladies are back!"

Indeed, they were. Lane carried several wrapped parcels from upstairs, her grandmother emerged from the parlour with some equally enticing packages, and most surprising of all came Alice, with several little things wrapped in brown paper.

"Right," Lane said. "Under they go. Now then, Ganf, those matches. Let's see how she looks in her full splendour!"

And she glowed and rippled with light when every candle was lit. The five of them stepped back to gaze.

Suddenly Alice, in a voice no one had suspected, began to sing. "It came upon a midnight clear, that glorious song of old . . ." Everyone who could, joined in. When the song was over, Mrs. Andrews let out a huge sigh. "That was lovely, Alice. I had no idea you could sing like that! Shall I cut us all a bit of that cake? And we'll want someone to play Father Christmas. What about you, Marc? You are our guest."

He smiled. "Yes. We call him Saint Nicholas at home. We even put real candles like this, all around. But electric lights are safer, no?" He went to the tree and pulled a parcel out, reading the label. "This is for you, Mrs. Andrews.

And this for Mr. Andrews. And this for the young lady. And something too, for Miss Lane. I am very sorry I have nothing to give."

"Never you mind! You will see something for yourself, Marc. Just there." Mrs. Andrews pointed toward the back of the tree and then fell upon her own parcel. "Oh, Lanette, my angel! But this is a luxury I do not deserve!" she cried. "Chanel!" She pulled the bottle out of the box and removed the stopper, breathing deeply. When she'd held it out for all to sniff, she hugged Lane.

"My dear girl," said Ganf. "Just the thing. My old ones are on their last fingers!" Ganf held up his new gloves. More hugs.

Marc had opened his parcel and was holding its contents to his chest, his eyes moist. "You should not have. Someone here will have need of it, no?"

"Not a bit of it. When I heard my granddaughter was bringing a guest for Christmas, I set to work. I hope it will get you through this beastly cold," Mrs. Andrews said.

Marc held out the scarf, knitted in moss green and some light blue like the sky, for all to see, and then wrapped it around his neck. "I will not forget this Christmas. Not forever."

Alice, who had put on her lipstick and thanked Lane with a little kiss on the cheek, said, "How about mine? This is for you, Miss Lane, and here is one for you, Mr. Andrews, and Mrs. Andrews."

Each parcel contained a little embroidered sampler with spring flowers and, incongruously, the word "Christmas!"

"Why, Alice, whenever did you have time for all this?

They are absolutely lovely! Did your mother teach you this?"

"Aye, she did." She could not suppress a pleased smile, but then turned with businesslike efficiency to the cake. "Is anyone going to eat this?" She began to pass out plates of cake. "I made it, you know."

Ganf carefully broke off a corner of his piece and chewed it, frowning. He began to nod slowly, as if his own senses had surprised him. "That, my dear Alice, is jolly nice cake!"

WHEN IT WAS over, the candles blown out, the kerosene lamps turned off, everyone sent to their beds, Lane and Ganf went to the back and checked the kitchen door.

"It is strange to be so happy when a sword hangs over our heads," he commented, testing the door. "Well, it's locked, but we've no bar to slide across it. A good kick would do for it, I'm afraid. I should perhaps have installed them on both doors."

"Why would you? No one expected that there would be a war and the enemy would be at our actual gates. I will sleep with my pistol, and I suggest you do the same with yours. I expect Marc has something. I haven't asked."

Ganf turned to look at her. "When did you become so wise and bossy? You are your father's daughter, and I say that with admiration. For all his faults, your father made us all feel safe. We're here because of him. I will not forget that soon. And I feel safe with you now."

LANE LAY AWAKE long into the night, fully dressed, her head full of images of the lights on the tree and the angelic sound of Alice's voice, together with visions of Freda, angry and somewhere out there with Rudy, ready to sacrifice everything for the Reich. She didn't feel like she could keep anyone safe at the moment.

It felt as if she'd only just gone to sleep when she was awake suddenly and completely, her heart pounding. She looked around in the dark, her hearing on full alert. There it was: an urgent whisper. For a moment she felt completely disoriented, thinking for a moment the whisper was in the room, but then she remembered her window. She always, even in the winter, cracked her window open a little. The whispering was outside. German. A woman's voice. Then a man's. They were here!

She threw her legs off the bed and crept to the window.

"They are asleep. We should act now because it will be more difficult to travel when it is light. Tell me about the inside of the cottage."

There was a longish silence. "Like this: kitchen here, hall, sitting room, library, stairs. I assume lavatory upstairs and at least two if not three rooms. The back door is farthest from where they would sleep. I don't think it is well secured."

"All right. Let me think."

Lane didn't wait. She picked up her shoes and stepped into the passage, her heart skipping when she nearly ran into Marc in the blackness.

"They are here," he whispered. He too was dressed. "We will be ready for them." Lane nodded, and then tapped on the door of her grandparents' room. Her grandfather was out in seconds.

"They're here," she whispered. "Outside my window. They are thinking of using the back door."

"We must wake Alice!" Ganf whispered urgently. "She will hear them where she is sleeping in the little room in the back of the kitchen, and she'll try to stop them. Now I wish we'd sent her home to her family where she'd be safe!"

Lane nodded. "Meet in the kitchen," she said, and turned and raced down the stairs, cursing the creaks in the wood. Marc followed her.

"Alice! Wake up!" She was shaking Alice gently and whispering.

"What is it?" Alice asked out loud, sounding groggy, as if she'd been in a deep sleep.

"Shhh!" Lane whispered. "Get your robe and get upstairs. Someone bad has come here. I want you safely out of the way!"

They were joined that moment by Ganf. "What if they try the front? I think we have to stay together if there are two of them," Ganf said.

Alice appeared from her closet bedroom fully dressed. She went to the stove and took up her iron frying pan. "I'll stand by the front door. I can get at least one of them. I'd not mind hitting that man again, if it's him."

Lane stifled a smile. "All right, Alice." Having her out of the kitchen would be much the safest. She had no doubt the attack would come at this back door. "But you stay behind the door. They will be armed, and there are two of them. We have to telephone the constable, but I can't do it just now. They'll hear."

"I'll do it," Mrs. Andrews said. In the dark they hadn't seen her come in. "I'll take the phone under the—"

At that moment, they could hear activity at the backdoor.

Someone was trying to open it.

"I'll go now!" Mrs. Andrews whispered. "They won't hear at the front." With that, she hurried through to the passage. They could hear the sitting room door close in turn.

"Alice, go with her!" Lane hissed, "And Marc, we cannot afford for you to be hurt. You must go with her as well! Don't argue, go. If they are armed, they will try for you first!"

After only a moment's reflection, he slipped into the passage and closed the kitchen door softly.

Lane tiptoed toward the back door with Ganf. They stood so that they would be behind the door when it opened.

They hadn't long to wait. With an explosion of sound in the quiet night, the door was kicked in, flying at them and ricochetting violently back toward the interlopers. Clearly, they'd given up on a silent approach.

"Now!" said a woman's voice in German. "Get upstairs before they have time to react!" Freda! Lane tightened her grip on the revolver and then loosened it, trying to relax. Two figures, mere shadows in the dark, hurried into the kitchen, and one of them turned on a torch.

"There," the man said, "the door."

They made for the door, but as Freda reached for the door handle, Lane and Ganf stepped out. "Put your hands up and drop your guns. I am armed," Lane said firmly. Startled, Freda and Rudy wheeled around, the torch falling to the floor so that its light illuminated the bottom of the stove. "Your guns, please. I warn you, Freda, I'm a very good shot."

"All by yourself, Lane? You can't take on two of us, and I don't think you'd shoot anybody. I know you, remember?"

She hadn't seen Ganf behind Lane in the dark. With terrifying ferocity, she flew forward hard into Lane, knocking her back against the kitchen table. Lane could feel a sharp pain in her hip where she struck the edge, and the table slid and crashed back into the wall. Something fell to the floor and there was the sound of breaking glass. Her revolver had flown out of her hand. She pushed her arms straight out to try to shove Freda away, but Freda had her hands around Lane's neck, her fingers like iron hoops, thumbs pushing against her throat.

So intent was she on prizing Freda from her throat that she could not hear the other commotion in the dark kitchen, weirdly lit now only under the cupboard where the torch had been kicked in the melee. Figures wrestled and jostled somewhere, angry grunts and banging in the dark.

Suddenly there was a shot. The sound tore through the room like a bomb, and for a moment everything stopped.

Lane could feel the thumbs letting up slightly on her windpipe. She gasped in some air and coughed painfully, feeling her throat tear. In the next moment, the scene was flooded with a blinding light. The electrics had chosen that moment to come back on.

Before Lane could close her eyes against the sudden glare, she gave Freda a final shove that sent her slipping sideways. As the burden of Freda's weight fell away, she sat up quickly, holding her throat with one hand and using the other to steady herself.

Everyone seemed to be in the kitchen. Marc was holding Rudy with his arms behind his back. Ganf stood looking at where he'd shot a hole in the ceiling. Alice was standing by the stove with the frying pan, and Mrs. Andrews was advancing on Freda. With a cry of rage, Freda was up on her feet, lunging at Lane again, who pushed the heel of her hand hard at Freda's chin, causing her head to snap back.

Alice, frying pan in hand, was about to go for a second act when Ganf stopped her and stepped in to slide Freda, still stunned, into one of the chairs that hadn't been overturned. "You stay there, young lady. Alice, put that down and see if you can get us more of that rope."

By this time, Marc had Rudy in a chair and was holding him there with a gun. There was a loud pounding on the front door.

"Don't get up," Mrs. Andrews said, smiling. "I'll get that."

CHAPTER EIGHTEEN

"**IN MY HOUSE, MY GRANDMOTHER** would say to soak a cloth in brandy and wrap it around the throat," Marc said.

"A shocking waste of brandy!" Ganf protested.

"Lots of honey in a hot cup of tea. The only thing," declared Mrs. Andrews.

"Enough!" cried Lane, waving her hand in surrender. Her throat felt bruised and hurt abominably, but she wasn't going to say so. "I'm perfectly fine. I'll take the tea with the brandy in it. And shouldn't we be thinking about the goose? Where's Alice?"

They were sitting by the fire in the stillness of a quiet Christmas morning. Outside, after days of snow-laden then rainy and overcast skies, the sun sparkled on mounds of new snow piled over the garden. Only the walk down to the road was well trampled by the nighttime comings and goings. Duncan had arrived at the same time as someone from the local Air Force base. They'd carried away Freda and Rudy, and everyone in the house had finally fallen into bed well past three.

"She's making breakfast. Porridge all around with toast, and she's bringing out the marmalade, as it's Christmas."

"Who made the marmalade?" Ganf asked nervously.

"I did," said his wife firmly. "No, Lane, sit down. I've already offered to help her. She said her kitchen has had enough disruption and she wants everyone to stay away."

Lane leaned back in her chair and took sip of tea, and felt, for the first time since she'd left London only four days before, something like a momentary contentment.

"WELL?"

"Well, what?" Barkley said. He disliked being put under pressure by this woman. Major Hogarth and her colleague Robert Finley from the Special Operations Executive had come to his office to quiz him. The SOE was some newfangled department of highly doubtful origin as far as Barkley was concerned.

"How did she do? You picked this woman for the job. I'm asking you how she performed," Hogarth said.

"She managed to stagger through, I suppose. She got our man, I'll say that."

"And managed to collar a homegrown female spy for the Reich, and a German spy whom we'd captured once, only to have this Freda Beauville set him free and go on a rampage across the border country." Shaking her head, she said, "Beauville's father got her a job as a typist on the deputy minister's staff, if you can believe it." She turned to her colleague. "And the safe recovery of Marc Nowak protects our entire intelligence network. I think I make my point, Finley. We need to recruit women. Deadlier than the male, you might almost say. Between the Beauville girl—who was very crafty indeed, for the wrong side, alas—and this

Winslow girl, we can see that we are underutilizing the skills this country has to offer."

"Look, we've got one woman out there now, that Granville woman. Let's see how she gets on before we go off half-cocked."

"I'll talk to Dunn." She wondered if it was he who had insisted on Lane Winslow. "I want an eye kept on Winslow. I think she's got what it takes. She's shown herself to be resourceful and courageous." She turned to go, and then turned back. "Oh, and Barkley, well done. I don't know who suggested you pick a woman, and her at that, or if you thought of it yourself"—she sounded skeptical of his ability to make sound decisions—"but very well done. A broken clock is right once a day, what? Now then. I think they've got some attempt at a Christmas lunch going in the mess. Shall we?"

Barkley gave a wan smile. It certainly hadn't been his decision. It had been the decision of someone much higher up the chain than either of them.

LANE'S THROAT WAS considerably improved by lunchtime, and she could just swallow if she chewed thoroughly. "Really, Alice, you've done a wonderful thing with this goose. I doubt we'll see such a good feast again till this beastly war is over."

"Yes, is very good," Marc said. "It is as my mother would make." He sighed. "God bless her soul."

Alice looked suitably serious for a moment, but then beamed. She turned to Lane. "Do you really have to leave, Miss Lane?" Alice's older brother was driving them to

Edinburgh in his lorry to catch the night train in a couple of hours.

Lane nodded ruefully and glanced at Marc. "We really do. But not before a little walk, and then brandy and more of that excellent cake." She lifted her glass, coughed a little, and then said, "Thank you, everyone, for everything. Alice, you watch, you'll be recruited into the army with that frying pan before you know where you are! Grandmama and Ganf, when I think what might have happened to you! I feel awful bringing such disaster to your Christmas."

"Absolute rubbish, my dear!" Mrs. Andrews exclaimed. "I've never enjoyed myself so much. I can't imagine a more exciting Christmas!"

LANE SETTLED AT her desk with the file of communications that had come in that morning and looked around at the other girls, and at the two men, who had the nice desks by the window. It was as if none of it had happened. She tried to settle into the familiarity, relish the relative safety of her occupation, but she found herself thinking about Scotland. It had been really exciting, she thought, discounting the hours of tramping and waiting in the bitter cold: the rush of fear when she found someone at the pickup ahead of her. Was she one of those people who thrived on danger? No. Of course not. She was not, she reminded herself, anything like her father. Her mood was down to the post-Christmas let down, and really, her job was a little . . . unvarying.

Lane turned and looked around, frowning. She'd felt quite bad about suspecting poor Irene of anything besides being nosy, where she hadn't suspected Freda at all. She wondered if it was prejudice because Irene had so clearly come from a modest background, and decided guiltily that it was. It was so easy to jump to conclusions about people on very little evidence. She'd not been surprised to find that Irene was not at the bedsit when she got home, but now she saw Irene's desk was empty as well.

She leaned over and asked the girl next to her,

"Where's Irene?"

"I heard she's been reassigned."

"Do you know why?"

The girl shrugged and then leaned closer and gave Lane a knowing look. "You know they don't tell us peasants anything. But she speaks German, doesn't she? I bet she's been sent out there to keep an eye." She giggled. "A woman spy . . . can you imagine?"

Well, thought Lane, well. Irene's essential nosiness put to good use. Maybe one day they would see sense and start using women for something besides this. She opened her folder, sighed, and got to work.

ACKNOWLEDGEMENTS

IN A WAY, I AM indebted to the BBC for this story. Fifty-six years ago, I was living alone in a London bedsit with my adorable brand-new baby who, to my dismay, arrived without instructions. As a respite from anxiety, I became addicted to BBC full-cast radio dramas. At the time there was a thrilling wartime story about German submarines sneaking to the coast of Scotland at night. Every evening, I sat rapt with cocoa and blanket. The whole thing had just reached a peak of suspense . . . the dark, the stormy sea, the flashing lights, the enemy paddling furtively toward shore . . . when I had to leave London to go home. Ever since then I have wondered how that drama ended, and no amount of scrabbling through online BBC archives has revealed the name of the story, nor any trace it. When the opportunity to write a prequel to the Lane Winslow mysteries arose, my first thought was "I have to finish that submarine story!" And of course, the incentive to discover a little bit about Lane at the age of twenty—indeed, my very age when I heard the story of the nighttime submarine invasion—was too delicious to pass up.

I am so grateful to my second family, TouchWood Editions, for the perspicacious and kind support they give to making my books ready for the world. Publisher Tori Elliott, who is a bubbly and enthusiastic supporter of Lane Winslow. My very skilled and patient editor, Nara Monteiro, with their editorial team of Claire Philipson and Kate Kennedy, all of whom seem to know exactly what to do to make each book the very best it can be, and always make me feel good by saying how much they enjoy them. A huggy thanks to publicist Curtis Samuel, a boon travelling companion, an unequalled planner of itineraries, and someone who knows where all the good bakeries are.

Special thanks to Rill Askey, the peerless and very popular narrator of the audio series, for her invaluable guidance on British expressions in this book, which takes place entirely in Britain. The books are beautiful to look at, and that is down to the magical art of Margaret Hanson, and the design team at TouchWood, including August Knibutat. A very special thanks to Pat and Rodger for their kindness and cheerleading for the Lane Winslow project.

I am braced by the support of my family; my husband Terry, who puts up with my doubts and enthusiasms with his own benevolent insight about the stories. I couldn't do without him. My son Biski, and daughter-in-law Tammy. My grandsons Tyson and Teo, a writer himself, both of whom put up with my pressing all manner of books on them. My brother and family, my nephews and cousins in England and France. Nothing but aye-sayers the lot of them!

PHOTO BY ANICK VIOLETTE

IONA WHISHAW is the author of the *Globe & Mail* bestselling Lane Winslow Mysteries. She is a two-time finalist for a BC and Yukon Book Prize, and has twice been nominated for both the Left Coast Crime Award and the Crime Writers of Canada Awards. The heroine of her series, Lane Winslow, was inspired by Iona's mother, who, like her father before her, was a wartime spy. Born in the Kootenays, Iona spent many years in Mexico, Nicaragua, and the US before settling into Vancouver, BC, where she now lives with her husband, Terry. Throughout her life she has worked as a youth worker, social worker, teacher, and award-winning high school principal, eventually completing her master's in creative writing from the University of British Columbia.

WEBSITE: IONAWHISHAW.CA
FACEBOOK & INSTAGRAM: @IONAWHISHAWAUTHOR

THE LANE WINSLOW MYSTERY SERIES

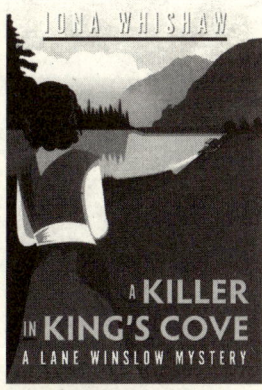

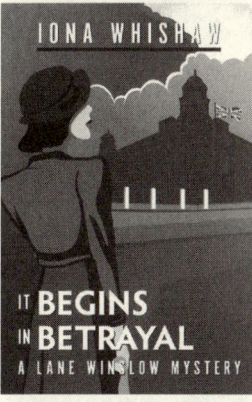

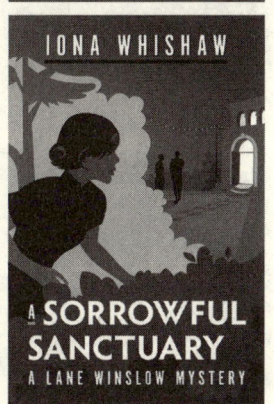

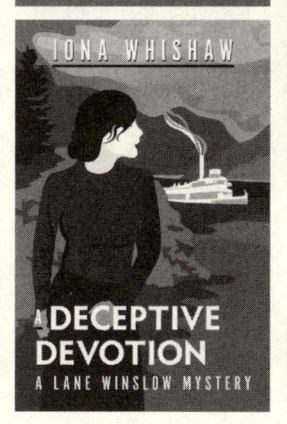

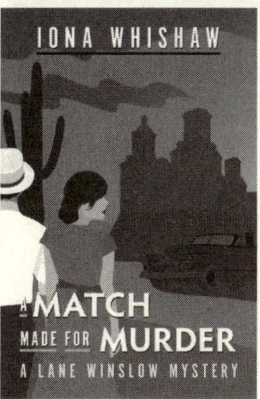

- A Season for Spies: A Lane Winslow Prequel
- A Killer in King's Cove: A Lane Winslow Mystery
- Death in a Darkening Mist: A Lane Winslow Mystery
- An Old, Cold Grave: A Lane Winslow Mystery
- It Begins in Betrayal: A Lane Winslow Mystery
- A Sorrowful Sanctuary: A Lane Winslow Mystery
- A Deceptive Devotion: A Lane Winslow Mystery
- A Match Made for Murder: A Lane Winslow Mystery
- A Lethal Lesson: A Lane Winslow Mystery

THE LANE WINSLOW MYSTERY SERIES

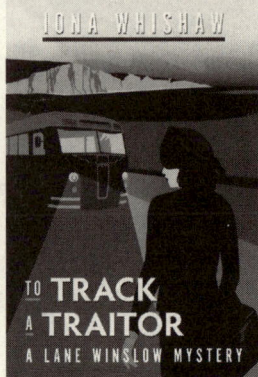

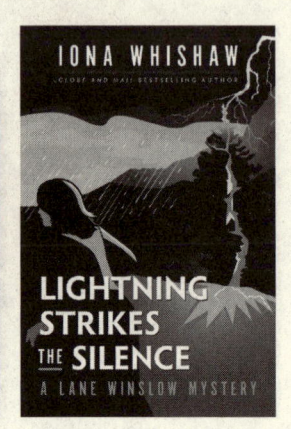

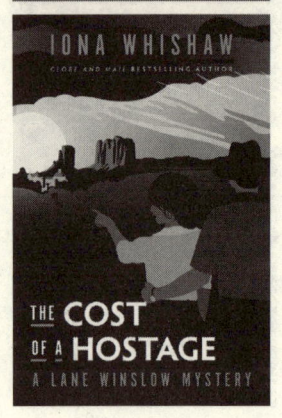